SHOOTING
SNAKES

SHOOTING SNAKES

MAREN BODENSTEIN

modjaji books

All the characters in this book are fictitious. Any resemblance to persons living or dead is purely coincidental.

Publication © Modjaji Books 2013
First published in 2013 by Modjaji Books PTY Ltd
Copyright © Maren Bodenstein 2013

P O Box 385, Athlone, 7760, South Africa
modjaji.books@gmail.com
http://modjaji.book.co.za
www.modjajibooks.co.za

ISBN 978-1-920590-01-7

Cover design: Tannah Stroebel at Life is Awesome Design Studio
Book design: Life is Awesome Design Studio
Author photographed by Graeme Williams
Printed and bound by Mega Digital, Cape Town
Set in Calisto MT

For Lizzi, Joppie, Trudel
and Hans Dieter

"And truly I was afraid, I was most afraid,
But even so, honoured still more
That he should seek my hospitality
From out the dark door of the secret earth."

from 'Snake' by D.H. Lawrence

1.

The prophet was calling from the hills. All night long he could hear her singing and praying. Calling and crying out, God knows what. It was enough now. Right in front of his house. He would have to go outside and tell her to stop. She could not carry on so. Not so near his house. Could she not think that he was trying to sleep?

Johannes sat up stiffly and fumbled at the alarm clock on the bedside table. Five-to-five. He sighed and lifted his legs over the edge of the bed, feeling for his worn-out slippers with his feet. Slowly he pushed up his body until he could feel his legs steadying beneath him. It was going to be a long day.

He shuffled along the dim passage and into the lounge. The room was still hot from yesterday. He squeezed his way through the thickset furniture and pushed aside the brown velvet curtains. Just as he had thought - she had made a fire in the dried-up riverbed. It was dangerous to make a fire in this drought – all you needed was a sudden gust and there would be a helluva veld fire. He had seen it happen often enough in the plantations around Witrivier.

At least the singing and praying had stopped for a bit. Leaning against the old car wreck, she was holding her face up to the red-brown dawn, the flames leaping towards the lower branches of the old blue gums illuminated her body.

Johannes turned around and walked towards the large sideboard. Avoiding the stern gaze of his parents from the picture on the wall, he rummaged in the drawers for the binoculars. That was the thing about getting old, you could never find anything.

By the time he got back to the window the woman was prostrating herself towards the rising sun, her black mourning cloth fluttering around her shoulders. Probably had lost her husband. Or her sister. She slowly lifted her strong torso against the firelight. Johannes held his breath. Her breasts were firm and round, he shouldn't be looking at her like this. But it was not as if he hadn't seen this kind of thing before, the heathen women in Venda often wore only a cloth wrapped around their waists.

She was beautiful. Like VhoSarah.

And then the dust from the curtains made him sneeze.

'Old man's bladder,' Johannes mumbled apologetically towards his mother and father as he pushed his way back through the furniture, barely making it down the passage into the dark bathroom. He watched with relief as the thin stream of hot brown urine splashed into the bowl.

The kitchen was warm and dark. As he waited for the kettle to boil, Johannes spooned coffee into his mug, one of the ones Kate had bought for their new house here in Stillefontein just before she died. And now the roses on it were fading already. She always bought things with flowers on them – bedspreads, cups, the curtains in the bedroom, even the lampshades.

The condensed milk was nearly up. He would have to go to town today. Johannes tried to stem the tide of irritability by switching on the radio, which blared loudly and then quickly died again. The batteries were flat. He could never remember to buy new ones. Anyhow, it spared him having to listen to the endless stories of crime and corruption on the radio.

He picked up his mug and went to the breadbin to fetch the heavy bunch of keys.

A rush of coolish morning air flooded into the passage as he opened the front door. The binoculars hung guiltily around his neck, he would have to be careful not to disturb her. Why was it that every morning there was the same struggle to open the damn security gate?

By the time he finally got outside there was no sign of the woman. Just the sky, which had taken on the merciless white-blue of a hot dry day. Johannes sat down stiffly on the rocking chair and savoured the rush of coffee through his body. The tin roof clicked from expansion and soon his irritation rose again. What was wrong with her, wailing and singing like that right in front of his house? Showing her breasts. Didn't she realise there was someone trying to sleep inside? Ever since boarding school he had struggled to sleep. Maybe he should go and report her at the Stillefontein police station. But it was no use. He could already see it - the sergeant at the desk friendly but subtly mocking him. And he would have to explain to him carefully that it was not the praying and singing that bothered him - he was used to that growing up in Venda; the place had been full of prophets and rainmakers and the Malombo women drumming through the night - no, it was the fact that she was making a fire so near his house that was wrong. It was dangerous, especially in this drought.

Johannes lifted his binoculars again. There was not even a trace of smoke from the fire, just a few stray cattle tearing away at the already powder-dry veld.

The snakes would be out today because of the heat.

A group of schoolgirls from Kareepan was walking along the path, chatting and laughing. They were wearing the white shirts and green tunics of Stillefontein High. At least now with the new government they could get a decent education. Father had always believed in a good education for the natives. Johannes just wished they wouldn't litter so. Threw anything into the veld. Didn't they teach them not to litter at school nowadays?

Foxy used to hate the schoolchildren. Ran a path all along the fence, barking. They'd teased him terribly, poor dog.

Sweat was running down his back and Johannes began to rock again, pressing the chair into the wooden floorboards. Beneath him the cellar, where the snakes were hiding. The week he moved in here he had opened the door to look inside and a rinkhals was hanging from the low beam, hissing at him angrily. He had never gone inside again. Susanna could mock him about this as much as she liked, but Jooste had told him that's what snakes did when it's too hot, go into the cellar under the house. Over the years his neighbour Jooste had killed about seven snakes in his own cellar.

"You must brick up that door," he had said, "then they can't get in."

Johannes got up to make himself another cup of coffee.

By the time he remembered that he had forgotten to feed the birds, the sun was already high up in the sky. Johannes climbed down the steep stairs of the veranda and made his way to the garage. It was dark and cool in there. He stubbed his toe against a bag of hardened fertilizer and cursed. He really had to tidy up in here some time - the shelves were full of things he had brought from the farm. It must be seven years ago already since he moved here. In those days he had still had plans to make a proper garden, but all he had managed to do was plant two peach trees and a few hardy marigolds that re-seeded themselves every year. Never had been much of a gardener. Not like Kate, she had had been the one with the green fingers.

As Johannes emerged from the garage with the little red cup full of seeds, he could see the birds waiting for him already. Fluttering down from the blue gums onto the razor wire, sitting on the lawn and crowded onto the branches of the peach trees, waiting for him to finish cleaning out the birdbath and fill it with fresh water.

Damn, Grace and her granddaughter Pulane were standing at the fence. Must have been watching him for a while already and he hadn't noticed them. The last thing he felt like doing was talking to anyone today. Besides, Grace was always asking him how he was and whether he needed help and telling him about her family.

The birds were hungry. He counted twelve sparrows, five weavers, nine pigeons, six doves and three black widow birds. And then the little swarm of blue waxbills, which always seemed to drop out of the sky from nowhere.

And each one shall be counted, it said in the Bible.

It was awkward. He wished Grace would move on.

"How are you, Pappie?" she called finally. "You have lots of birds coming to feed today?"

One thing you had to say about Grace was that she always looked tidy and formal. Even in this heat she was wearing a maroon beret, a blue skirt and a white long sleeved blouse. She had told him some time ago that she used to be a nurse.

"Slept badly," Johannes confessed, despite himself.

"It's hard to sleep in this heat," Grace said sympathetically.

"No," he pointed to the blue gum trees. "It's that woman. She keeps me up all night."

Grace looked towards the trees, puzzled.

"She makes a fire and prays and sings and dances all night."

Grace laughed. "You're lucky Pappie, it's six weeks already no rain and the rainmaker is visiting you!"

Johannes noticed a blue plastic bag dancing next to the fence, skipping along the path and off into the veld. Pulane noticed it too and started chasing after it, zig-zagging, squealing with pleasure as she tried to catch it. Just as she got close, the bag rose up into the air, higher and higher until it nearly vanished. The little girl laughed and clapped her hands. Slowly the blue bag glided back down again and settled right on top of the razor wire where it began a crazy, blue, billowing dance, trying to free itself.

It was getting hot and besides he couldn't spend the whole day out here watching plastic packets. Johannes greeted Grace and slowly made his way up the stairs and into the kitchen where he boiled the kettle for another cup of coffee. He was so very tired today.

Once it was safe again, Johannes went to sit outside on the rocking chair. Even out here on the veranda it was unbearably hot. The plastic bag hung limply on the wire now. Johannes shook his head and started to rock. Harder and harder he rocked, kneading the planks with his chair. Beneath him the slithering mass hiding from the heat.

Father is interned

Father says that one of these days he is going to be arrested. Mutti and he discuss it all the time. Since Jan Smuts joined the war many German men in South Africa have already been put into the internment camps. There's even a camp in Salisbury in Rhodesia for the women. Father has written a letter to the area police commissioner explaining to him that he cannot leave Wittenberg because he has to be there to keep the mission station and the school running, but he says he doesn't believe that it will help that much.

Always when we are eating he remembers something else he has to tell Mutti in case he is taken away.

"Evangelist David will take over the congregation here. You don't have to worry about him, he is a solid Christian. You can also trust Teacher Lalumbe, although sometimes he loses his temper too easily."

Father is prepared.

The policemen come to visit Wittenberg every month. They come in a car. There are two of them. They have brown uniforms and pistols in leather holsters. Father speaks to them in English and he invites them in for tea. Mutti takes out the best teacups and her ginger biscuits. She can't speak English.

Last week I had my birthday. I am six now. I always have my birthday around Easter. Anna is only going to be five in October. Even though Father says that the summer is over, it's still very hot today. So Anna and I are allowed to ask Samuel to take the tin bath to the garden and fill it with water. We splash each other. Willie is still too small. He is lying in the basket on the kitchen veranda. Mutti is baking bread. Willie has to be near her because he drinks milk from her. Father says we are not allowed to watch.

Anna ducks under the water and comes up with a mouthful and sprays it all over me. So I also duck under, but when I come up I see that the two policemen are standing there watching us. Anna has her back to them and starts to splash me again. They were here just a few days ago and I wonder why they are back already. Why don't they go straight to the house? Anna splashes harder. "What's wrong with you,

Hannes?" she asks.

Then she turns around and sees the policemen behind her. She is embarrassed and quickly dives back under the water. A few drops splash the one policeman's neat khaki pants. I think he is going to be angry but he just smiles and puts his hand into his pocket and takes out a handkerchief.

When Anna comes up to breathe the other policeman holds out a tin of toffees with silver wrapping. Anna quickly gets out of the bath and takes a whole handful. I only take two. Asta is barking at the policemen. She only has three legs because her one leg was caught in a trap. Father wanted to shoot her but Mutti stopped him.

Anna runs off into the garden with her sweets. I take off my bathing costume and put on my shorts and shirt. The policemen wait patiently for me. Their shoes are shiny.

I take them to Mutti. It is very hot in the kitchen and smells of fresh bread. When Mutti sees us she doesn't offer to make tea, instead she grabs the sweets out of my hand and walks to Father's office, which is at the end of the passage outside the kitchen. The policemen follow her and they go into Father's office. I can see he is angry.

I go and stand next to Mutti. Father calls her inside and when she comes out she is pale. She goes straight through the kitchen to their bedroom and opens the cupboard and starts to pack.

"It doesn't make sense," she says angrily. "Here in Africa, Christian nations should be standing together."

When I try to help her, she says, "I think it'll be better if you go outside and fetch Anna."

Willie is crying in his basket on the back veranda. I try to make him quiet and then I run to the garden to look for Anna. She is sitting in the treehouse. She isn't supposed to be there. Father built it for me, but Mutti says she is too small to understand that and I must just let her. But I know that Anna knows very well that it is my treehouse. She is always stubborn like that. Now she refuses to come down.

"They are taking Father to the camp," I tell her.

"They can't," she says. "He has to look after the mission station. He said so."

"But they are still taking him."

Slowly she slips down the steps that are nailed along the big trunk of the tree. When Father hammered in the long nails, Anna asked him whether it would hurt the tree and he shook his head and said that some trees only bear fruit if you hammer nails into them.

Anna is taking her time to come down, so I run inside again without waiting for her.

The policemen are throwing all the clothes out of the cupboards. Even Anna's and mine. They are looking for something. Father is shouting at them in English. I wish he wouldn't. What if they do something to him?

"I am a man of God," he mumbles in German and turns to Mutti and tells her all the things she needs to do when he is away. Who to contact, what building needs finishing and which outstations need special attention.

"I know Wilhelm, I know," Mutti says impatiently. "We have gone over all of this already. And I've got the list you made."

"I will be back soon," he tells me. "You'll see. This war won't last long. Germany will win soon."

Anna is standing at the door to the bedroom. Father smiles at her. "You be a good girl now. Do what Mutti asks you to."

He kisses her on the forehead.

"Where are they taking you?" Anna asks.

"They'll probably take me to Andalusia, the big camp near Kimberley."

"Are they going to hurt you in prison?" Anna asks tearfully.

"No," says Father. "It's not so bad. They just want to keep the Germans in one place because of the war."

"But why?" asks Anna.

Father turns towards me: "Little man, look after your mother and sister and brother."

I think he is crying but I don't know. I thought that fathers didn't cry.

The policeman who had given us sweets is telling Father to hurry up. I hate him. We all follow Father and the policemen to the black car. One of them holds the back door open for Father to climb in.

"You can't take him away," Anna tells the policeman as he settles into the driver's seat.

"They don't understand German, darling," Mutti says.

Father waves at us from the back of the car. Mutti doesn't wave back. She is holding onto our shoulders, but Anna and I wave hard, like a waving machine, till the black car vanishes among the trees and down the hill.

When we get back into the house Mutti sends me and Anna to call Sarah and Wilhelmina. We run as fast as we can down the hill to their mudi. Tshamato barks at me, but Sarah calls him and he wags his tail. She is sitting against the big muomo tree braiding something. There are two girls playing next to her. Wilhelmina is sitting on her mat talking to a boy, but Father says we are not allowed to play with him.

I'm just about to say something but Anna is already explaining. "The policemen have taken Father away to the camp in Andalusia in a big black car and it's near Kimberley where there are diamonds but it isn't too bad because there are a lot of other Germans there with Father and we have to call you to come to the house."

When we get back to the house Mutti is busy tidying up and Willie is crying. Wilhelmina picks him up and gives him to Mutti so that he can drink.

"Just give him some water," Mutti says. "I don't think I've got much milk."

Sarah takes us to the kitchen and cuts some fresh bread for us. She puts lots of butter and jam on. When Mutti comes into the kitchen her face is tight: "I have a terrible headache. I'm going to lie down," she says. "And Sarah," she looks stern, "we mustn't spoil the children while the Mufunzi is away."

When it is dark, Sarah puts Anna and me into bed. She sits on Anna's bed and sings to us for a long long time. Somewhere in the night I can hear drumming.

When we wake up, Mutti calls Anna and me into her bedroom. The curtains are closed and it is dark. She says that she is not feeling well. She has a terrible headache because she is very angry that they have taken Father away. She tells us that we mustn't forget that she and Father love us both very much.

"But now you must go to church with Sarah and Wilhelmina. Evangelist David is conducting the service today." Mutti sighs again as we leave the room.

"Don't forget to lock the chickens up. I don't want those monkeys to get hold of the eggs and chicks while you're all at church," she calls as I close the door.

Anna and I put crush in the feeding trough and then we run around the garden and chase the rooster into the coop. Soon the hens follow him in.

2

Somehow the day had passed, like so many others, and Johannes never did get around to going to town. He had made do with a small packet of sugar that he found in the back of the cupboard to sweeten his coffee.

The flies were really bad, probably had something to do with the drought. They came over from Jooste's dairy. He had complained to his neighbour about it often, but Jooste just shrugged his shoulders.

"Sorry man," he had said good-naturedly. "Dairies attract flies. There's nothing much I can do about it."

The flypaper in the kitchen was almost full. Maybe he should buy some fly spray instead. Although the palegreen fly swat worked well, you just had to sit still for a while and then you could kill quite a few. Always surprised him that flies have blood.

The people from Kareepan were walking home already - cleaners, gardeners, shop assistants - their day's work done. Johannes wondered how they still had the energy left to laugh and talk like that after a full day's work and in this heat. It was a long way from Stillefontein to Kareepan, but they would have their reasons for not taking the taxi.

He too had worked hard in his day. Got up early every morning to go and fetch the labourers with the bakkie. Worked every day of the week. Weekends he would inspect the pine plantations before breakfast and the rest of the day he would do repairs and maintenance.

They hadn't complained much, Kate and Susanna. They just got on with their lives. Maybe they were relieved when he got into the bakkie to check the pine plantations. Guess he hadn't been much of a father or husband, but he did support them - at least no one could hold that against him. Susanna got to go to a very good private school in Swaziland. He had even managed to pay for her university studies. He had had to make his own way through agricultural college. Father could never have paid on a missionary salary. He couldn't really compare himself to Father though,

Father had achieved things. Been part of the larger picture, part of history. Built churches and schools and a clinic, translated hymns into Tshivenda and Sesotho. Even when the Mission Society closed down Wittenberg, he had gone on to establish a theological seminary for young black pastors.

He and Kate, on the other hand, had lived a more quiet life and stayed in their little house on the farm till it was time to retire. Kate had dreamed of leaving Witrivier and living in Pretoria, retiring there. She said she wanted to spend more time with Susanna. She was going to join a gardening club and make a new rose garden. The climate was perfect for that in Pretoria, she had said. Then one day he had seen this place advertised in the Farmer's Weekly. It was a bit far from Pretoria but the estate agent had assured him that there was a strong vein of water running through the plot.

"You're practically buying the 'fontein' of Stillefontein," he had said. "It's perfect for growing fruit and vegetables."

So he had bought this place without even going to look first. Hadn't told Kate either. She had been so angry with him - she never showed it, but he could tell. They had been living together for thirty years already. Then after a while she had said that it would probably be okay. "Roses love hot summers and freezing winters," she had said. "As long as you promise to put up the borehole immediately, Hannes."

But she never got to plant her roses. Packed up their house and then, a week or so before they were supposed to move, she had died. A thrombosis. He had been so angry with her for not holding out a bit longer. He had looked forward to them being here together. They could have gone for long walks with Foxy, maybe even got to know each other a bit better again. At least he would have tried to explain to her why he couldn't live in Pretoria; about there being too many memories. She would have grown to like this place in her own way. It was quiet here. Even though everyone from Kareepan walked past the house, at least no one bothered each other really.

Just the snakes. He'd found another rinkhals basking on the garden path soon after he saw the one in the cellar. Father used to shoot snakes, would just fetch his shotgun and shoot them. But he, Johannes, didn't have the stomach for that.

It was time to go inside. Johannes got up abruptly. Tomorrow he'd stop by at Jooste's on his way to town and ask him to brick up the cellar door. It would at least stop any more snakes from getting in. Johannes locked the security gate behind him and made his way through the passage towards the kitchen. This time of day always affected him, like he was expecting VhoSarah and Mukegulu to start lighting the lamps. Maybe he should listen to the seven o'clock news. He turned the black plastic knob of the radio but the crackling reminded him that the batteries were flat. Couldn't really remember either whether he had eaten anything today. There was some canned food in the cupboard but he couldn't read the labels, the light was too dim. Ever since Susanna had replaced all the globes with those energy saving ones he couldn't see properly in here.

At least the light in the fridge worked. There was an open can of chilli pilchards and some apples inside, and a half-eaten slice of jam bread on a saucer - probably had made it earlier. It would just have to do.

A fly lay buzzing on its back on the kitchen table. Johannes reached for the fly swat and nearly knocked over the old brass paraffin lamp. One of the old ones from Wittenberg still. He had brought it into the kitchen a few weeks ago when there was a power cut, but he knew it was dangerous to keep it in here, could easily cause a fire. They were getting more and more frequent nowadays, the power cuts. Made you wonder about the new government. Father had always predicted that they wouldn't be able to run the country.

Johannes took the saucer with the jam bread out of the fridge. Maybe he could try to sort through Father's papers tonight, he had always inspired people. Got things done.

The spare room was stuffy and hot. Johannes pushed aside some of the agricultural magazines and papers that were spread over the bed and sat down. Maybe he should move in here. It was probably much cooler than his own bedroom because of the veranda. It protected you from the sun and you could open the windows easily. Susanna could always use his room when she came to visit. It was much bigger. She never came more than twice a year anyhow, too busy.

He looked through the faded flowery curtains into the dark night. From here he would be able to watch that woman. Make sure she didn't burn down the place. But there was no sign of her tonight, just the shrill sound of cicadas.

Johannes pulled out the wooden kist from under the bed. Father had made it when he was in the camp. Johannes opened it and sat down on the bed again, looking though the familiar contents – reports, journals, correspondence, surveying instruments, maps, plans, the chess set Father had made in Andalusia. A folder with letters - to Mutti, to his family in Germany, to his missionary colleagues in South Africa and Germany. He had been a remarkable man, you could say what you wanted about him but Father had lived his life to the full. Always knew exactly what to do. Not like me, Johannes thought, constantly wondering if he had done the right thing and forgetting what he was supposed to do.

There was a yellow folder he had never seen before. Johannes switched on the dusty bedside lamp. Old exercise books that belonged to Susanna. He wondered how they had got in here with Father's things. Kate had probably put them in here.

"Susanna Weber, English Composition, Standard 9". She had got good marks for composition. Not like him - he had always struggled with words.

My Family
"Once upon a time I was swimming in the warm circles of my pool. I was with all the other fishes - freshly spawned, blood-red pearls streaming from the motherbelly. Deep warm dark pool, swimming, swimming in circles, touching gently, streaming, diving deep and shallow, dipping, circling touching.
And then suddenly one day I was spewed onto the dry land of Mother, Father, No Brother, No Sister. I found that I had become a Daughter."

Strange words.

The teacher had written in red. "Very good Susanna. Maybe you can turn it into a poem. Just mind your handwriting. 8/10"

He had never understood her properly, his daughter. Always thought she didn't like him, from when she was small; she was always angry with someone or something - with the government, with Father, with farmers – she hated farmers – but mostly with him. Still, it was a pity to let all this lie here and gather dust. He had phoned Willie from town a while back and asked if he wanted the kist, but Willie said that he wasn't interested in the past. Maybe he should take it to the station and send it to Susanna in Johannesburg by train. She could fetch it and decide what she wanted to do with it all.

Johannes went to sit at the little desk in front of the window, took out a pen and paper and stared into the darkness. Then he wrote:

My Dearest Susanna,   *21 November 2010*

I would like to send your Grandfather Weber's things to you by train. Please let me know if that is all-right with you and to which station I should send them to. They are in the kist he made in the camp. Maybe one day, when you have time to read what he has written, you will understand your grandfather a little bit better.

With Best Wishes
        Your father
        Johannes Weber

Johannes looked at the letter for a while and then put it in an envelope and sealed it. He had never been any good with words.

Mutti tells us stories

Mutti doesn't want to eat. Wilhelmina scolds her. Every time she fetches the tray from Mutti's room, she says "The Mufunzi won't be happy if he hears that you don't eat and stay strong." For a long time now Mutti has been lying on her bed under the mosquito net. She looks beautiful with her long black hair all loose. Usually when it is winter the mosquito net is packed away but now Mutti refuses because she says it makes her feel safer. She doesn't like it when the Malombo women drum all night. She says it makes her restless.

At night Sarah puts us to bed. She doesn't tell stories as well as Wilhelmina but she sings beautiful. Afterwards she goes and sleeps in the kitchen on the floor. The kitchen is nice and warm from the oven. Anna keeps asking why Sarah doesn't sleep in a bed, but she just laughs and says that that is how the Tshivenda do things.

Sometimes after breakfast, when Mutti is feeling well, Anna and I are allowed to go and sit on her bed and watch her feed Willie under the mosquito net. Mutti doesn't mind. Sometimes she tells us stories and other times she asks us a lot of questions: "Are you remembering to pray for your father?" Or "What is Samuel doing? The Vendas can be lazy, you know." Sometimes she asks us whether Sarah and Wilhelmina say bad things about her. We tell her that they are not saying anything bad.

"How did the Mission Society expect us to support our husbands if they didn't even let us go to language school so we could learn African languages?"

Mutti scolds us when Anna and I talk Tshivenda to each other. "Your Father is not sitting in a camp for Germans so that his children can turn into little Vendas," she says crossly. She also doesn't like it if we go and play too far away from the house.

"It is important that we stay together," she sighs. "The Vendas have been known to kill children for body parts."

Anna and I look at each other.

But sometimes, when Mutti is in a good mood, she reads us stories from the big fairy tale book or she just tells us things. We sit under the mosquito net with her.

"You can come inside my tent," she says and we crawl under the net and snuggle up next to her on the pillows. Anna says Mutti smells of milk and apples. She tells us the story of little Red Riding Hood who went into the forest and met the wolf.

"You mustn't go into the forest, children," she says, "because here in Venda there are even more wild animals than in Germany."

"Tell us how you met Father!" Anna likes that story most.

"I always wanted to serve God," Mutti smiles. "Ever since I was a little girl I dreamed of continuing the missionary work of my father in India."

Anna and I settle next to her on the bed. Mutti's hair is long and loose and her skin is pale and soft. She looks like Snow White in the storybook.

"When my Mutti died of malaria I was only a little girl - like you, Anna." Mutti strokes Anna's hair. "Soon afterwards we children were sent back to the mission orphanage in Berlin. The three of us, your Uncle Paul and Aunt Irma and I got onto the big steam boat with Fraulein Schaefer and sailed all the way round Africa and back to Germany." Mutti sighs. "And your poor grandfather stayed behind in India. By the time he died, they say he had only managed to convert twenty-three souls. Those Hindus were even harder to crack than our Vhavenda. But at least they didn't drink."

"I wish I could go on a big ship to Germany."

"I am sure one day, Hannes, you will."

"Me too! Me too!" Anna always wants to do what I want.

"Oh my little Anna, one can never know where life will take one." Mutti is sighing a lot nowadays. "When we stopped that time in Durban on our way back from India, I never thought that, one day, I would be back to marry a missionary."

"But how did you meet Father?" Anna says.

"I was the only girl from the children's home to be accepted as a teacher trainer." Mutti sits up a little now. "I was still studying, when one day I went to a talk by one of the young missionaries who had just come back from Africa and was travelling from congregation to congregation, telling people how they could contribute towards the church's mission effort. At the end of his speech he joked, 'And if there are any strong young ladies out there,' he said, 'just remember that life is hard in Africa for us missionaries and we need good wives. Suddenly I knew what I had to do. I was going to volunteer to be a wife to a missionary. The next day I took the tram to the mission society headquarters to make enquiries. They interviewed me and were very impressed."

Mutti brushes through her hair with her hand before continuing. She looks beautiful, like a bride with the mosquito net all around her.

"There were five young mission candidates in Africa at that time, looking for a wife. Each one had written something about themselves and about what they were looking for in a wife. There was also a photograph. I was drawn to your father's picture with his wild curly hair and clear, intense eyes. But when I read his passionate description of his work as a missionary, I immediately knew that this was the man I wanted to marry."

Willie is making a noise in his sleep and Mutti puts him down at the foot of the bed and covers him with a blanket.

"A year later, after he had finished his language studies and done his practicals, your father picked me up at Durban harbour. He was much shorter than I had expected." Mutti laughs. "Shorter than me!"

Anna wriggles around with pleasure. She can never sit still.

"But I still thought he was handsome. Later he told me that when he saw me on the pier he thought that this tall skinny woman didn't look tough enough for the work at Wittenberg."

"Tell us about the wedding!" Anna is impatient.

"We had a lovely wedding. It was at Pastor Schroeder's house in Durban. My father had sent me a beautiful piece of raw silk from India and I had had a dress made in Berlin. Frau Schroeder had made a veil for me."

Mutti has shown Anna and me her wedding dress. She keeps it in a box in the bottom of her cupboard wrapped in white tissue paper.

"The only problem was that Frau Pastor Schroeder had forgotten to bring the veil to the room where I was getting dressed. She was so busy cooking and getting things ready and there I sat, waiting and waiting for someone to bring it."

"And then you cried, didn't you Mutti?" Anna looks at Mutti and moves in closer to her.

"Yes, I cried," Mutti says softly.

"What happened next?"

"Next, we did the three-day train journey to Pretoria. Missionary Els and his wife picked us up with their new car. He was the first missionary from the North to have a car. On the way to Wittenberg we had to stop three times to visit all the mission stations! Your father wanted me to meet his colleagues and their wives." Mutti sighs. "I couldn't wait to finally get to our own mission station here at Wittenberg."

Anna is playing with the mosquito net. "And what happened then?" she asks impatiently.

"I had always thought that Africa was only savannah and thorn trees, but when I got to Wittenberg I found a beautiful green place with mountains and thick forests. I was so surprised. And the house was much grander than I had expected. And everything so overgrown. Your Father called it Sleeping Beauty's castle. It was the grandest mission house that the Berlin Mission Society ever built in South Africa."

Mutti loves telling this part of the story.

"Missionary Bester had first built the mission station at the bottom of the hill near the river where the malaria mosquitoes lived. When Old Wittenberg caught fire, he went to Germany to raise money to build a new house and the Mission Society even commissioned a famous Berlin architect to design them a prototype. Firstly, it was built much higher up on the mountain. The architect designed the house with high ceilings and a large veranda all around to cool the place down. It was also the first time that a mission station had its own slaughter room with a storeroom to keep the meat fresh."

Mutti sighs again. "In Venda everything rots so fast."

"And then? What happened then?"

Mutti smiles at Anna. "You won't believe the mess this place was in when I arrived! Wilhelm had just got here a few months before and had tried his best to make everything ready for me, but during his three-week absence things had already turned wild again. The mice had moved into the pantry and a bird had died in our bedroom. I got such a fright. It was being eaten by the largest maggots you have ever seen."

"Yuck!" I say.

"Poor Wilhelmina had especially slaughtered a rooster and boiled it. She had also made maize porridge."

Mutti sits up and shakes off Anna who is playing with her hair. "I wasn't used to this kind of food, and as soon as I got into our bedroom that first night I was sick all over the floor."

Poor Mutti.

"What made it worse was that that night your father had to prepare a sermon because the Bishop was coming for a visitation. So he only came to bed very late and it was so dark at Wittenberg and I was very afraid. I just couldn't sleep. And the drumming, the Malombos were drumming non-stop. Every time I lit a lamp one of these huge nectar moths would come flying at me and I thought it was a bat."

Anna flies past my face with her hand.

"Stop that Anna!" I say.

"Not so loud, Hannes," Mutti admonishes me. "You will wake up Willie."

But Willie only groans a little in his sleep.

"Nobody had warned me about the insects in Venda!" Mutti continues. "On the way here we had stopped in Louis Trichardt and bought a nice piece of roast for our first Sunday lunch. I wanted to make a good impression on the Bishop and we had invited the Els'. When I woke up that Sunday morning to put the roast into the oven it was half eaten by the biggest ants I had ever seen."

Mutti picks Willie up before he starts to cry. She pulls down the front of her nightdress and presses his little mouth against her nipple. He sucks. The room smells of milk. I lie against Mutti.

"Not so close, little man," she pushes me away a little. "Willie is very sensitive."

I don't like Willie. He has a red face. Mutti says he looks like Father.

"When you were still in my tummy, Hannes, all I wanted was soft white rolls, fresh from the bakery in Berlin and butter and milk that didn't taste of strange grass and herbs."

The room is nice and warm now. Anna is starting to wriggle and I can see she is getting tired of listening.

"It was a daily struggle to get food on the table - and I wanted so much to impress your father. So it often ended in tears." Mutti laughs. "Just as I was eyeing the lovely fruit in the orchard, the monkeys would come and bite into the mangoes and then discard them, half eaten. Once I had specially saved some white flour so that I could bake your father a birthday cake. When I opened the bag, the worms had spun a thick web inside. It was horrible."

Anna tries to stare out of the window through the net. "Can we take Willie for a walk in his wagon just now?"

"And the heat - I thought I would die," Mutti continues. "There is no gentleness here in Africa. When the sky is blue it is so bright and when it rains it rains hard. This place just doesn't care."

She wipes the sleep from Willie's eyes.

"Mutti?"

"What Anna?" Mutti says irritably.

Anna doesn't ask again.

"I can't have you going outside all the time. And besides it's too cold and there are witchdoctors who kill children so that they can eat them."

Then Mutti chases us out of the mosquito net because she wants to rest a bit.

3

It was all a big mess. Already in the aeroplane flying low over the smudged and dirty skyline of Johannesburg, Susanna had wished that they would somehow be forced to turn around and head back to Tanzania. She certainly didn't feel like going home to her townhouse with its high walls and neighbours who never greeted her.

When she finally pulled up in front of her garage door, after endless passport controls and waiting for luggage, the remote didn't work. She pressed it again and again, but it still wouldn't work, so she climbed down from her seat and went to open the heavy door manually. The electricity must have tripped. She was so tired, hadn't slept at all on the aeroplane. Not that she was a good sleeper at the best of times, but her mind had been racing after all the drama at the conference.

Susanna heaved her suitcase out of the boot and rolled it along the unevenly paved path. The front garden was weedy and dry. Where had David been? She had paid him extra to come twice a week to keep an eye on things.

As she unlocked the front door, a terrible stench hit her. It came from the kitchen. The fridge. When she opened it she saw rotten apples in the vegetable draw, and the deepfreeze was a stinking slosh of defrosted spinach, peas and tofu burgers, and who knows what else. The lasagne had turned green and fungal. Shit! The mains must have tripped during a thunderstorm or something. Why hadn't David reported this to the caretaker?

She should have listened to herself and not come back here. She had longed to stay on in that little village in Tanzania with the dilapidated German mission station that reminded her so much of Wittenberg. After losing her temper at the conference with those post-colonial pricks from the First World countries who thought they knew everything, she knew it was time to take a break.

The lounge looked so tatty with papers and journals lying around. The floral covers of the easychairs that Mom had given her were fading badly. She would have to replace them. Susanna was drawing back the heavy curtains so that she could open the door to the little garden when there was a loud knocking on the front door. What now?

"Oh Miss Weber, you are back," the caretaker said. He was a large nervous man who seemed to start sweating and blushing as soon as he spoke to her.

"That man who was supposed to come and look after your place, he never came."

"I can see that."

"And you didn't leave a key with me."

"I gave my spare keys to David."

"And now Mrs Daniels from number 12 says he is dead. He used to work for her as well, you know."

Shit.

"He died two weeks ago." The caretaker turned even redder. "Probably AIDS, you know?"

"Yes," she wanted to say, "in your eyes they all die of AIDS."

"Thank you," she said.

"Is your electricity back on?"

"Yes, it tripped." She wished he would go away. "I'll probably leave again this afternoon, visit my father in Stillefontein. I'll have spare keys made before I go so that Lena can clean the place."

"It's better you give the keys to me."

"I will. I will." She closed the door after him and sighed.

When she had unpacked her suitcase and thrown her dirty clothes into the washing machine, Susanna listened to the messages on the answering service. There were a couple of frantic calls from David's sister who said she needed money. He'd only worked for Susanna for three months, but he had been pleasant enough and seemed to really enjoy gardening.

Susanna lit a cigarette and went to inspect her little garden. The succulents she had collected on her field trips in the Richterveld had all survived, but many of the pelargoniums had not made it. And the pond, oh the pond! Of course, the pump had not worked with the tripped electricity. Her beautiful pond with its filtering plants and the talapias she had collected and the wild little yellow waterlilies, had turned into fish soup. She needed to get out of here quickly.

Her face looked sickly against the beige of the bathroom tiles. She got in the shower and washed her hair. Avoided looking in the mirror while she dried herself – at the skin that turned bright red at the slightest whiff of heat, hair that was ready to spring back into an unruly mass of ginger blonde, and short fat legs and arms. It was just her luck to look like Grandfather. Grandmother and Auntie Anna had been so beautiful – tall and elegant with beautiful long black hair in their youth. Mom had been plain, but at least she was never fat.

As soon as the first load of washing was done, Susanna went off to the mall. She parked her car at the car wash - at least they could clean her car.

After Ethiopia and Tanzania it was a pleasure to be in well-stocked shops. She headed straight for Woolworths. It was important to stock up on delicious things when she visited Dad – good coffee, Belgian chocolate biscuits, cheeses, pasta sauces and good olive oil. Stillefontein didn't offer much retail therapy and his cupboards were usually completely empty.

There was still time to go to her favourite coffee shop for a quick mega-cappuccino and a cigarette. She had stopped smoking eight years ago but after her disgusting performance at the conference in Tanzania she had started again with a vengeance. It calmed her down a bit and maybe she could lose a bit of weight this way. And stop chewing her bloody nails.

She'd have to phone Althea soon and face the music. The room had gone deadly quiet after her outburst at the conference and for the rest of the time there everybody avoided her or was too polite. Althea would be angry with her. She wouldn't fire her but she would be very angry. It didn't help that they had broken up just last year.

By the time she had finished packing, dumping the rotting food into the outside bin and given the keys to the caretaker, it was already afternoon. Susanna locked the front door. Maybe she could just leave this mess forever. Go and live at the sea or something - she had wanted to live at the sea ever since she was a child.

Exhaustion swamped her body – she would have to stop for a bite and more coffee. It was madness to drive in this heat, but at least she had aircon and the CD player and her gorgeous big Subaru. She'd had it for two years already. The love of her life!

As soon as the Joburg traffic eased off a bit, she phoned Enquiries and asked to be put through to the B&B in Stillefontein. She couldn't face seeing Dad yet, maybe tomorrow or Wednesday. While she was negotiating with the puzzled owner that a proper vegetarian meal and a bottle of red wine were to be brought to her room, Althea called. Susanna ignored the call. She didn't feel quite ready to talk yet. She had sent Althea a cryptic e-mail from the airport in Dar es Salaam explaining why she had lost her temper at the conference.

This stretch of road outside Vanderbijlpark was so ugly - kilometres of squatter camps on the outskirts of the industrial heartland. Susanna put on her favourite CD - 'Women of Mali'- but after half a song she switched it off again. She needed to be quiet.

Going to that mission station in Tanzania had reminded her of Grandfather in his black Luther robe. He must have been holding a sermon somewhere. They had been driving for a long time and she had so looked forward to seeing her grandparents. She ran up to Grandfather who held out his hand to her in formal greeting and said to Dad, "Why are you not teaching this child any German, Hannes?"

And typical Dad, he had just turned away.

Susanna dialled Althea's number. She might as well face her wrath, but the phone was on voicemail. Instead she called David's sister to find out what had happened to him. The woman was distraught, she said David had had a sudden bout of pneumonia and died.

"Did he have AIDS?" Susanna asked.

"No. Pneumonia." His sister hesitated. "We need money to pay the undertakers."

"David only worked for me for a short time."

There was a long silence. Why do the poor always spend so much on funerals? Susanna softened. "I'm not in Joburg. I had to leave again for work," she lied. "Is there a bank account where I can deposit some money?"

There wasn't, so she said she would arrange with Althea to give the family some money. The sister could go and fetch some at her office in Braamfontein on Wednesday.

Things were looking terrible – even the drought-resistant strains of mealies looked bad and the cattle even worse.

When she stopped at the Ultra City, the heat pushed hard and dry against her, so she fled into the Wimpy and ordered a vegetarian burger and coffee. Maybe she should just book into a motel in Klerksdorp, take some sleeping pills and sleep for a couple of days. Forget everything - Tanzania, Dad, Grandfather, Althea.

As she got back onto the M16, Althea called.

"How you doing?"

"Fine." Susanna lit another cigarette.

"What happened in Tanzania?" Althea's voice was cool.

"Everyone was being such arseholes." Susanna could feel her anger rising again. "They were using the same old stupid arguments - reintroducing culling to sponsor nature conservation. I can't take it anymore."

"You know that some of our funders were there?"

They were both silent for a bit.

"Do you think I should take a sabbatical?"

"Brilliant idea," A sigh of relief. "Get that PhD proposal going."

"Did I fuck up badly?" Susanna inhaled deeply.

"You know there are people who would love to see you fired. You really need to work a bit on your people skills."

"I know."

"But it's a good idea you take a break. Take care of yourself."

Suddenly there was a bump under the tyres. Through the rear-view mirror Susanna could see the bloody mess on the road.

"Shit!"

"Are you okay, sweetie?"

"I just killed a banded mongoose." Susanna could feel tears welling up.

"Why don't you go and stay with my mom on the farm? You always liked it there. Take as long as you need, Susanna. Phone me if you need to chat."

Susanna hung up and hooted angrily at the Black-shouldered Widowbirds feeding on the verge of the road.

"You're going to get killed," she shouted at them.

She'd forgotten to ask Althea about giving money for David's funeral. She'd have to call her again. Maybe she could persuade her to come and visit her in Stillefontein, it would make Dad more bearable.

The caterpillars started. There were hundreds of them crossing the highway. Susanna pushed the hooter hard. Stupid suicidal creatures crossing the boiling hot tar! She hooted and hooted. A local farmer overtook her, flashing his lights at her, looking at her incredulously.

Susanna opened her window and shouted: "What's your case?" and pressed the hooter again. Then she swerved the car off the road and came to a halt under an ugly old bluegum. Her hands were shaking. She finished her cigarette in a few deep draws and shut her eyes tightly.

We have a picnic at the river

Late in the afternoon, when Anna and I come back from playing in the pine forest next to the church, we find Mutti standing in the kitchen. She is excited.

"Uncle Els was here," she smiles. "He went to Louis Trichardt yesterday, and guess what?"

We don't know.

"He brought back a letter from your father!"

Mutti's face is shining. There are flowers on the kitchen table. She is frying potatoes and making eggs with spinach – our favourite.

"It's time you got some healthy food again," she says.

Before we eat she asks Sarah and Wilhelmina to come and sit with us around the kitchen table so we can translate for her.

"Hannes, please tell them that the Mufunzi has written a letter from the prison."

It's getting dark in the kitchen and Mutti lights the paraffin lamps. Then she sits down and smooths the tablecloth in front of her. "He says that I must not neglect all of our spiritual needs. And although I've never really been taught how to, I am going to learn to pray in front of other people."

Sarah and Wilhelmina smile and nod at Mutti encouragingly. Mutti looks through our children's Bible and reads us the story of the prodigal son. Then we sing a hymn together and the brass lamps shine brightly.

"Vhafunzi Weber is a good man," Mutti's voice is a little shaky. "We have to keep his work going here at Wittenberg."

We all sit in silence for a while.

"Tell Sarah and Wilhelmina that if they hear of any women who are sick around here they must let me know. I don't want those Malambo women to get hold of them. I'll go and pray for them myself."

When Sarah and Wilhelmina have gone home, Mutti reads Father's letter to us.

My Dearest Elisabeth,   *12 September 1941*

Finally they have organised through the Red Cross that we can send letters home. We are each allowed one letter a month but maybe around Christmas I will be allowed to send an extra one.

I must say the journey from Pretoria to Andalusia was very long. There were only four other Germans with me on the train. Just imagine, we had a whole carriage to ourselves with five military policemen looking after us. They are really wasting good money on guarding us. When we got to the camp we were each given a khaki uniform and allocated a barrack. I am sharing a barrack with eleven others, mostly decent men. Some farmers from South West and Natal, and a very cultured wool merchant from the Eastern Cape who loves to play chess. The only problem is that the barracks get very cold in winter and very hot in summer. Soon when it is summer we will have to start bribing the guards with cigarettes to allow us to keep the doors open at night. Lately we have had an infestation of lice and so we all had to have our heads shaved and clean our barracks with disinfectant every week. We look like real prisoners now.

Every morning at seven we go out onto the parade ground and do exercises. We are not allowed to sing any German marches or folk songs; instead they hoist the British flag and we have to salute it. Otherwise our camp commander is a very sympathetic man, a real English gentleman. He has told us that he is merely following orders and that as long as we obey the rules he will not make our lives difficult.

I have joined the choir (a male choir of course!). At the moment we are already preparing for Christmas, practicing our arrangements of Advent songs and carols. I am really looking forward to Brother Eiselen's sermons. He is here in the camp with us and is supposed to be one of the best theologians in the country.

What is truly a blessing is the number of missionaries and pastors that are interned with me here at Andalusia. Quite a few of them are also fine theologians who have started a theological university and are offering courses. They are following the syllabus of the university of Berlin and are negotiating for our studies to be accredited through the university. At last I will have the opportunity to deepen my studies and get a proper degree! I have already enrolled for four subjects, including Systematic Theology, Practical Theology and Pedagogy and have to do a lot of reading before we begin in January. Also, we have set up a discussion group on missionary work in Africa. This will prepare us for when we return to our mission stations and congregations. It is so wonderful to share ideas with my Brothers in Christ. In January we are going to hold a seminar about saving the soul of the African from the powers of witchcraft, and I am delighted to have been asked to share the difficulties we are experiencing among our Vhavenda in Wittenberg!

Please send kisses to my beloved children. Tell them that we even have a professional baker from Windhoek who is interned with us and I bet we will have some fine German Christmas cakes this year!

My thoughts are with you constantly, and don't forget amongst all your troubles to look out for the spiritual well-being of our little family.

Your ever loving husband,
Wilhelm

P.S. I forgot to say that if you have any problems with meercats or snakes don't hesitate to ask Maharaj to organise a hunter to see to the matter.

On Sunday after church, Mutti declares, "It's such a beautiful spring day, let's go to the river for a picnic!"

We pack food and a blanket into Willie's wagon. Wilhelmina has roasted a chicken for us and prepared a delicious potato salad. It has pieces of green mango and macadamia nuts in it. We also take a tin of Mutti's ginger biscuits and lemonade.

Mutti is still a little bit weak and the river is far, so we have to take turns to carry Willie on our backs.

When we get to Old Wittenberg, we rest a little under the big wild fig tree next to the graveyard. This graveyard has more people buried in it than in the one above our house. Mutti says it's because in those days people didn't know that mosquitoes caused malaria and that living down near the river gave you the fever. Mutti says we can't go inside the ruin of the old house because it's dangerous.

"Why?" I ask.

"It burnt down and it isn't stable."

"How did it burn down?" asks Anna.

"I'm not sure. They say it was struck by lightning. One of those Venda superstitions."

We want to hear the story and Mutti tells us that it happened when Missionary Bester was away on a mission trip. Luckily his wife and children had gone to visit relatives in Pretoria. The heathens said that it was because the missionaries had cut down a mvula tree to build the house. It was Raluvhimba who sent the lightning bird.

"Uncle Els says that the heathens believe that the ancestors are helping to clean out the poison that has come to the land." Mutti gets up and we continue walking towards the river. "They mean the white people of course."

We have to be very careful not to slip down the embankment. Mutti says it is a pity we can't teach Asta to pull the wagon for us and we all laugh. Suddenly Mutti stops and draws us close to her. She says she's got a little secret to tell us.

"Uncle Els told me that soon every mission station in the North is going to get a car," she announces. "He says it's to help us to continue our work while our husbands are in the camp."

"Can I drive it?" I ask, excited.

"No Hannes," Mutti laughs. "Uncle Els is going to teach me how to drive. And then we can go on outings every Sunday and visit people."

When we get to the river Mutti spreads the picnic blanket under a huge jackal-berry tree and lies down with Willie. It's hot and she says that Anna and I are allowed to put on our bathing trunks.

"Can we swim without our trunks?" asks Anna.

"No," Mutti says firmly. "You aren't native children."

Anna and I run to the river and splash water at each other. The water is cool and clear and soon we are jumping up and down in the rock pool and making up silly rhymes. Even Mutti laughs. When she has fed Willie we go and sit by her on the blanket and eat our food. Mutti says Anna and I have to watch out that the monkeys don't come and steal it.

After lunch Mutti sends us off to collect flowers. We bring her lots of white trumpet flowers and she says that they remind her of Father's trumpet. When we have collected enough we lie together on the blanket and Mutti makes us each a crown for our hair. "You are my angels," she says and hugs us.

And then she tells us stories about life in Berlin with all its shops and streetcars and the university and the many people. "You can buy so many fine things in Berlin," Mutti looks dreamily into the distance. "There are shops everywhere where you can buy the most delicious cakes and chocolates and so many different types of breads and ices made of berries."

The talk of all the food makes us hungry again and we eat the cookies and drink lemonade.

After a while Mutti falls asleep on the blanket with Willie. She sleeps for a long time. Anna and I pretend to be the king and queen of Berlin and we rule with lots of chocolate and justice. When we are too hot, we go and splash in the shallows, careful not to wake Mutti up. Then we go and wee on the smooth river sand.

"Look!" I say. "I can make ribbons on the sand."

"I can't," Anna giggles, slipping off her bathing costume. "But I can make flowers. Look here, I made a big, big flower in the sand."

Mutti wakes up, startled. "Didn't I tell you to keep your costumes on?" she says.

"But I had to wee," Anna replies.

"Never mind," Mutti sighs. "It's getting late and we must hurry home."

On the way back we help Mutti to pick some flowers from the Old Wittenberg garden for our house. When we get home Wilhelmina and Sarah are already lighting all the lamps and making supper. Before they go back to their mudi we sing hymns and read from the Bible and pray together. Anna and I nearly fall asleep against Sarah.

"Tomorrow morning," Mutti announces, "I am going to call Evangelist David and Paulus. They are going to help me finish building the new schoolroom that the Mufunzi started. After that we are going to build the storeroom."

When we have eaten our supper, Mutti fetches the keys to Father's study. She is going to look for a book on Tshivenda grammar.

"You'll see, children," she says. "Soon my Tshivenda is going to be just as good as yours."

4.

There was always such a lot to do before he could leave the house. First he had to feed the birds, then look for stamps for Susanna's letter. But of course he couldn't find any. Then he had to look for the keys to the bakkie. Lock the house. Open the garage. Unlock the big stubborn gate.

At least the bakkie started after only two attempts. The battery was still strong it seemed. He should have mentioned in the letter to Susanna that she should take the bakkie when he dies. It was a bit old, he had bought it in Witrivier, but it was a much better vehicle than that old VW Beetle she drove. He had told her that it wasn't safe to drive around in such an unreliable car especially for a woman, but she had snapped at him, told him that she didn't want to be part of consumerism.

By the time he reversed out the gate Johannes was already sweating, straining his neck to check that no one slipped through the gate into his yard. Suddenly there was a scraping sound and he braked sharply. The rear-view mirror on the passenger side had hit the gatepost. He got out to check - wasn't too serious, just a bit of silver paint on the mirror. Johannes got back into the bakkie and reversed a few metres further so that he could close the gate. Then he remembered that he had forgotten Susanna's letter on the kitchen table. He made his way up the stairs again and unlocked the front gate, checking all the time that no one was stealing the bakkie.

Johannes stood in the kitchen for a while. Maybe he should put on a clean shirt while he was here, a cooler one. But it was no good washing his clothes too much, it just wore them out. He locked everything up again and got back into the bakkie.

With the roads so dusty he couldn't even open the windows. Besides, the window on the driver's side always jammed. He would have to have that seen to before Susanna took over the car. The road was getting a lot worse, more rutted. No one fixed things nowadays.

A woman was walking towards Jooste's farm, holding up a bright pink umbrella against the sun. He didn't know her.

Johannes glanced at the seat next to him where the letter was lying. Foxy used to sit there and stick his head out of the window and bark. Always barked at the people walking along the path. Wonder why? Guess Foxy hadn't been around people enough. They had lived a pretty isolated life at Witrivier, he and Kate. Hardly ever had visitors. The labourers didn't come onto the yard much either and Kate had done all her own cleaning. He never liked having servants around the house. It made things so complicated.

The veld was dry and brittle. There was no grazing to be had. Just a few goats nibbling at the leaves of a young thorn tree. Jooste was probably buying supplementary feed by the truckload already. He should call him from the Post Office and talk to him about bricking up the cellar door. Not a bad sort, Jooste. When Johannes had first come to Stillefontein, Jooste had invited him to the hotel for a drink. But he had never been any good at those things. All those people made him nervous and, besides, liquor either put him in a bad mood or made him feel sad.

Johannes leaned over to open the passenger window. The letter slipped down onto the floor. The wind blew hot against his skin. Maybe it was a stupid idea to go to town today. Susanna probably wouldn't be interested in Father's kist. What did he really need to do in town, besides buy a few groceries? Find a woman? Johannes snorted bitterly. With his thin, leathery body, where would he find a woman? The trouble with driving was that it could make you think about all kinds of silly things.

A few weeks before he married Kate he had panicked, thought he should probably learn something about it all. Couldn't talk to Willie about such things so he had asked Kate's brother. They had been to agricultural college together. He took Johannes to a big house in Pretoria, to the maid's room in the backyard.

"She can teach you a few tricks," he had said conspiratorially.

She had been a sweet woman. He had been surprised at the gentle mat of pubic hair, at the softness of it all. It had been a short and greedy event.

It was silly to even think of reporting that prophet woman to the police. She was grieving for someone.

Suddenly the bakkie stuttered and came to a halt. Johannes tried to open his window, sighed and turned the key in the ignition. Nothing. He got out and bent down stiffly to see if anything was leaking. He never was any good at fixing cars.

Johannes got back into the bakkie to pick up the letter. He shouldn't have left home today, now he would have to walk all the way back to Jooste's farm. The sun was burning white, he should have at least brought a hat along. Probably hit the sump on one of those ruts.

Then he saw Jooste's bakkie coming towards him in a cloud of dust. What a luck! Jooste stopped immediately. There were large patches of sweat on his neighbour's two-tone shirt and his tight shorts revealed his strong legs. He was obviously taking some young bulls to the abattoir. Too expensive to keep feeding them in this drought.

"Morning, neighbour," Jooste's grip was strong, like a real farmer's.

"Hell man but it's already hot this morning," he said. "And not a sign of rain."

He lifted the heavy bonnet of the bakkie with ease. Johannes stood next to him feeling his skin burn from the sun. Jooste's helper, Wiseman, was tending to the bulls on the back of Jooste's bakkie and lifted his hat in greeting.

"Funny how life works, hey. My wife was just talking about you this morning at breakfast." Jooste looked at the engine and quickly pulled loose a pipe. He bent down to suck at it, spitting out the petrol. Then he wiped his mouth with the back of his hand and closed the bonnet again. "This motorcar needs a good service," he said. "Your petrol pump is buggered."

He wiped his hands and neck on a greasy rag. "Tell you what, I'm just on my way to town. I'll tow you down to BJs. They'll fix it for you."

Jooste and Wiseman worked fast and effortlessly and soon they had linked the vehicles with a chain.

"Let Wiseman steer your bakkie and you come with me. Haven't seen you for a long time."

Johannes wanted to protest, but the sun was burning him and he obediently folded himself into the passenger seat next to Jooste.

"Sometimes we wonder if you are still alive there in your pondokkie."

Wiping the sweat off his face with his sleeve, Johannes turned around anxiously to see if his bakkie was okay. Wiseman waved at him reassuringly.

"You must come for a braai sometime. One of my boys can fetch you and take you home again." He winked at Johannes. "The wife can be a bleddie good cook when she feels like it."

The smell of the young bulls on the back, mixed with the greasy rag was making him feel sick. He could feel Jooste's sideways glance on him.

"Are those snakes still bothering you?"

"I meant to ask you." Johannes' tongue was heavy. "I want you to close the cellar door. Brick it up." He shooed away the flies that were buzzing around him.

"Don't worry, man. Snakes can't open doors." Jooste laughed. "Besides, there aren't many snakes left around here," he added. "They've all been killed. People are too scared of them."

Jooste reached over to pat him on the back and Johannes pulled away. "Anyhow," Jooste said, "my wife was saying this morning that we should organise you a cell phone or something. You can get them cheap nowadays. It's no good you don't even have a phone, how will we know if you're okay?"

They turned onto the tar road leading into Stillefontein and Jooste started to whistle a tune and then he hooted at a taxi that had stopped abruptly in front of them to pick up a passenger. Soon they pulled into BJ Motors and by the time Johannes had managed to climb out of the bakkie and stretch his legs, Jooste was already explaining to the mechanic what was wrong with his vehicle and Wiseman was packing away the chain.

"Doesn't sound like a serious problem, Mr Weber." The mechanic was a young man. "You can come back in two hours."

"Thank you," said Johannes and started to walk towards the Post Office, the letter in his pocket. Only when he was right in front of the building did he see the long queue of people snaking from the lawn up the stairs and through the doors. Just his luck to come here on pension day.

Johannes looked towards the old women sitting on the lawn, surrounded by children, talking, exchanging news. Maybe he could find Mukegulu among them, ask how Thambulo is doing? Sit down for a while.

He put the letter back into his top pocket and walked away. He would go and wait in the bank, at least there was air conditioning. Maybe he could sit there for a while. But the security guard asked him politely what transaction he wanted to do and guided him to the correct queue. Johannes withdrew some money.

When he emerged back into the bright sunlight he made his way to the supermarket. There he picked up a green shopping basket and started to walk along the aisles, unable to remember what he needed. Always forgot to make a shopping list. In the end he put a loaf of bread, ginger biscuits, bananas and a tin of coffee into his basket.

"Hullo Mr Weber." It was the manageress. He hadn't noticed her come up to him. "Haven't seen you for a long time."

"I'm looking for stamps," Johannes said.

"You'll have to go to the Post Office for that." He knew that. Before she could say anything else he turned around and made his way to the till.

A paper seller smiled at him and he wanted to explain that he had stopped reading the papers long ago. They just upset him because of all the nonsense that was happening in the country with the new government. Father had predicted all this chaos long ago.

He decided to try the CNA, sometimes they sold stamps. It was cool inside and the lady at the counter looked friendly, but she told him that she couldn't sell him one stamp only. He had to buy a packet of ten. Johannes thought for a while and then decided to take ten stamps. They had tropical fish on them. Susanna would like that.

This time he managed to squeeze through the crowds and get to his post box. He bent down and unlocked it. Never got much mail – just bank statements every month or something from the insurance. Sometimes there was a newsletter from the Berlin Mission Society which he always threw away immediately. In the end they hadn't treated the missionaries fairly, just closed all the mission stations in Southern Africa. They said missionary work was too much part of colonialism. They called themselves liberation theologians, or something. But what had made Father most angry was that some said that the missionaries should ask the Africans for forgiveness for destroying their own religion. Maybe they were right, somehow. But Father never lost his fighting spirit.

Among the junk mail there was a postcard with usambara violets on it. Someone must have put it into the wrong post box. That always happened. People weren't trained properly nowadays. But it was from Susanna, from Tanzania, posted three weeks ago. On it she had written she was coming to visit him.

Johannes didn't know what to do with the news, so he went back to the supermarket and bought more groceries. His legs were tired by now and there was so much to do suddenly with Susanna coming. He would have to clean the house and tidy up.

Maybe he could ask the mechanic whether he would let him sit in his office. Let him rest there for a bit till the bakkie was fixed. Or maybe he should buy himself a bright shirt from one of the hawkers on the pavement. Susanna would like that.

I see the **Holumbe**

Anna always pesters me to let her come up into the treehouse but I tell her that Father built it for me, not for her. Anna messes things up and she asks so many questions. I wish Asta could come up, but she can't climb trees because she only has three legs and because she is a dog. She lies at the bottom of the tree panting, waiting for me to come down.

My treehouse is high up and from here I can watch everything that is going on. The church is not so far from our house. If you walk along the path to the forest above the church you get to the graveyard where Missionary Bester's family are buried. Mutti says they all died of malaria, except for the Evangelists who died of smallpox. Mutti has also had malaria but she did not die. She just gets headaches and sleeps a lot. Mutti says she thinks that she is getting malaria again and it is making her sick all the time. We don't see her much at the moment.

On the other side of the church is the mission farm and below us live the Venda Christians. Each family has been given some land to farm and for that they have to send someone from their household to help on the mission farm. When Father first came to Wittenberg, the mission farm was completely overgrown.

"Just three years without a missionary and the place had already gone wild," Father told me.

But he soon got things in order again. He worked day and night, clearing, building and supervising. He fixed the vegetable garden and the orchard and loved pruning the trees. He built pens so that the pigs and the chicken were safe. Often when there was a commotion in the night he used to go out to shoot a meerkat or a cobra. There are many snakes at Wittenberg, but the worst is the black mamba. Father told me that once you have looked a mamba in the eyes you have seen death.

From up here I can see Wilhelmina boiling the washing on the fire. Sometimes she makes soap in the big black pot with pig fat and soda. Sarah is polishing the back veranda with Willie on her back. She is singing, always singing. Sometimes she and Wilhelmina sing together. It's beautiful singing.

This morning Anna asked me if I thought that Mutti is going to die of malaria - like our granny in India. She asked if she could sit with me in the treehouse a bit and I told her to go away, so now she is playing in the garden near the front door. It's where all the important guests go in but since Father went to Andalusia there haven't been so many visitors so nobody uses the front door. Only Djambo is there really, but he's just a head with no tusks. Apparently Missionary Bester had to have him shot because he was destroying our garden.

There's drumming coming from the mudi far down in the valley. The young girls must be practicing. I wish Mutti would give me some money so I can go to Maharaj to buy some sweets. I'm not allowed to go alone though. Mutti says I've got to be a bit bigger.

Anna is busy collecting things. She's not so sad anymore, it seems. She talks to herself and laughs. She says she's playing with the Holumbe, but I don't know what that is.

"The Holumbe is my friend," she says.

She seems to be playing with the Holumbe all the time nowadays. Even when it rains. She says it lives in the front garden and that the sunbird is teaching it to fly and that it lives inside Djambo. But when I ask her what it looks like, she says it looks funny-like. "Something like a rabbit or a big soap bubble," she says.

"Stop lying!" I laugh at her.

"It's got arms and legs," she explains.

Asta is whimpering so I climb down. Anna's thick black hair is full of leaves and flowers. She is making patterns with cigarette flowers in the mud and talking to the stupid Holumbe again. When she sees me she just ignores me. Then she starts to laugh.

"What's so funny?" I ask.

"Can't you see? The Holumbe is sticking its tongue out at you."

"It's not!"

"Careful," Anna is laughing so hard she has to hold her stomach. "It's right in front of you. It's going to lick your nose just now if you're not careful."

Asta is looking where Anna is pointing and wags her tail, but all I can see is a group of red dragonflies hovering over a puddle.

"You see, even Asta can see it," Anna says.

"You are telling lies!"

"Shht." Anna presses her fingers against her lips. "The Holumbe doesn't like it when you are too noisy." Anna leads me to some overhanging branches near the wild jasmine. "Look there," she whispers. "It's the Holumbe's nest."

"But you said it lives with Djambo. And that is a sunbird's nest anyway."

"Sunbird made the nest for the Holumbe," Anna explains softly. "It's made from spider webs, and has moss and flowers in it. Now the Holumbe can sit there if it wants to."

"You put those flowers in there."

"I didn't."

"If the Holumbe is big like a rabbit, then how can it fit into the sunbird's nest?" I try to catch her out.

Anna doesn't reply.

Then suddenly I can see the Holumbe! It is a silly creature with a big see-through belly and long arms and legs, which it flails about madly trying to stay in the air. It's right near the big cactus imitating the sunbird drinking from the moonflower. It looks stupid.

"Careful, you are going to fall onto the cactus," I shout.

"Don't shout," Anna whispers, "The Holumbe is still learning to fly and if you give it a sad thought, it crashes down onto the ground and starts to cry. Sometimes it cries just like Willie."

"It's stupid."

And then the Holumbe lands right in front of me and bursts into tears.

"See what you've done!" says Anna.

"Why is it crying?" I ask.

"It's very delicate," says Anna.

I don't like it when Anna uses those fancy words that she gets from Mutti. The Holumbe looks at me suspiciously between sobs and then it goes and sits inside Djambo's skull and falls asleep.

"Djambo is the Holumbe's best friend," Anna tells me.

"Well I don't care. Djambo was very bad to trample down all the fences and the orchard."

"He was very, very angry," Anna says. "His whole family was shot by the hunters, right here at Wittenberg. Just imagine if the policemen had shot Father and Mutti and Willie, what would you have done?"

"I would have killed them."

"You see," says Anna. "That's why Djambo is always in a bad mood."

Suddenly the Holumbe starts to giggle, then it laughs and you can see the laugh inside its tummy, black like a little swarm of bees. It grows bigger and bigger and then it doesn't want to stop at all and its tummy gets so big from laughing that it starts to lift off out of Djambo's head and flies without moving its arms.

"What is the Holumbe laughing about?" I ask.

Anna shrugs her shoulders. The Holumbe goes higher and higher above the trees. Just as we're getting a little worried that it will never come back, it lands right inside Djambo's skull again.

5.

By the time Susanna pulled into the B&B in Stillefontein her eyes were gritty and burning from the car's air conditioner. It was an old-fashioned place with crocheted doilies, dried flower arrangements and fans running wild on the ceilings. By the time she had dragged her suitcase up the stairs and into the room, she was sweating profusely. The room smelled of disinfectant. She pulled open the thick floral curtains and saw a little kidney-shaped swimming pool in the garden below. She could always move in here if things got difficult with Dad, which they invariably did.

The pool was lukewarm and heavily chlorinated. She lay on her back and looked at her white body floating in the water, the rolls of flesh she hated. The sky was a browny-pink and the mosquitoes were buzzing around her head, waiting for her to settle.

She woke up. The radio clock next to the bed was flashing 3.07. Served her right for drinking more than half a bottle of that Nederberg Cabernet Sauvignon that had immediately dumped her into a heavy sleep. But now she was wide awake. Susanna got up to open the window to let in some cool air but closed it quickly as a swarm of mosquitoes seemed to have been waiting outside, ready to enter the room. She turned on the ceiling fan, but it was too noisy. So she put on her costume to go for a swim. The security gate was locked for the night. What was wrong with these people? She smoked a cigarette and stared into the night.

She must have fallen asleep somehow because when she woke up again it was 6.45. The bedroom was stuffy from smoke and she pushed the ashtray and plate with last night's leftovers into the passage outside her room and opened the windows. The smell of baking bread seeped in through the smoky room and she could hear the rattling of cutlery in the kitchen. Susanna put on her swimming costume, thinking she should swim early before the sun became too hot. The security door was unlocked and outside the air was coolish, but the pool didn't seem to have cooled down over night at all. It was the temperature of pee.

After breakfast Susanna asked the manageress if it would be okay to stay another night. She couldn't face Dad just yet. The woman seemed a bit out of her depth dealing with a vegetarian. What should she cook for Susanna tonight?

"Room service is fine. Just make the same as last night, maybe change the vegetables."

Susanna went up to her room to put on her boots and a long-sleeved khaki shirt over her T-shirt to protect her from the sun. She felt like walking around Stillefontein a bit; transfer the money for David's funeral to Althea's account and maybe get a few more things from the shops. Knowing Dad, he'd probably not got her postcard yet. He hardly ever went into town. It was a constant mystery to her what he ate.

As soon as she stepped out of the B&B and the heat hit her, she regretted not taking the car. She wove her way along the pavement trying to stay on the shadier side of the wide, deserted suburban street. A posse of dogs yapped and barked at her from behind their large suburban gates. At least people didn't build such high walls here as in Johannesburg.

"Hullo Tannie," a group of blonde and barefooted primary school girls in dark blue tunics greeted her. Susanna was too taken aback to return their greeting and as soon as they had passed her she could hear them giggle. The main road was busy - people everywhere, cars and taxis, litter. Traders were selling shoes and caps and handbags and there were the ubiquitous Chinese shops with a range of colourful dresses hanging outside, blowing in the breeze. A man walked up from behind her and Susanna froze. Gold chains dangled from his dark arm. She couldn't understand what he was saying. He was definitely not a local. She shook her head.

About five young men in black uniforms, carrying large automatic rifles, were guarding the queue at the Post Office that wound across the lawns. It must be pension day. There were old people everywhere - talking or silently bent into themselves, some accompanied by their children or grandchildren, probably hoping to get something out of the meagre pension. An old man coughed into his handkerchief. Loud music blared from a street barber's tent, lovely gospel music. Women with large cooking pots were selling plates of food to the pensioners. Traders had laid out their goods on the lawns - second-hand clothes, vegetables, seawater, medicine in half-jack bottles, sjamboks, 'I love Jesus' wall hangings. She would love to speak to the women selling medicinal bulbs and plant materials but first she had to go shopping.

The little dusty supermarket was friendly enough but hardly stocked any fruit and vegetables besides onions, tomatoes, pumpkins and a few apples and over-ripe tomatoes. When leaving the store Susanna was accosted by two children begging for money. In principle she never gave money to beggars, so she reached into her shopping bag and handed over the loaf of bread and a litre of milk.

It would be strange if she met Dad in town today. She'd tried calling him several times on the cell phone but a woman's voice announced that the number she had dialled no longer existed. He'd probably forgotten the PIN number again and had let the SIM card expire. It drove her mad - how was she supposed to keep an eye on him if he couldn't even operate a cell phone? Or, more likely, if he didn't want to be accessible.

The heat was unbearable, all she wanted to do was lie on the bed at the B&B and read a newspaper. The CNA stocked a pile of two-week-old Mail & Guardians. It would just have to do the trick, fill her in on what had happened while she was away. At the till she picked up a bar of chocolate and some chips. Might as well eat.

That night she didn't sleep that much better either, so when she heard the security gate open in the morning she got up and packed her things. On her way out she bought a loaf of fresh bread from the owner – that, with cheese and jam and a strong brew of Woolies' Mocca Java, would be great for breakfast. Dad would like that.

As soon as she turned off the main road towards Jooste's dairy, Susanna could feel her stomach tighten. Things looked worse than she had remembered them. The veld was overgrazed and every single tree, with the exception of a few ugly old blue gums, had been chopped down for firewood. The road was badly rutted. Susanna could feel the familiar anger flooding through her body. What had gotten into Dad to buy a piece of land in this godforsaken place, and without even consulting Mom or going to see it first? He had always been so secretive and stubborn. The old car wreck was still rusting away in the ditch and she had a strong urge to turn back, but there was no use. He'd probably already spotted her from his chair on the veranda. Sitting there, just as she had left him six months ago, rocking away, watching the world through his binoculars.

At **Bester's** Graveyard

Samuel and I are planting beans and cabbage today and once we've finished we're going to tie rags on sticks so the birds don't come and eat the seeds. He's making holes in the soil and I'm allowed to put the beans in, but have to be careful because the beans are soft. Samuel left them in a tin with water through the night and the outside skin is coming off. He showed me where the stem and leaves are going to grow from.

Anna keeps running past us. She's trying to keep up with the Holumbe. It's flying up and down looking very pleased with itself. She says its flying got better since I also became its friend.

Once the beans are in Samuel and I put a warm blanket of soil onto them so they can rest and push their way through the soil to the sun. Samuel says we're all looking for the sun like the seeds, and when I look up at the sun, I can see the Holumbe high, high up - a little speck in the sky.

"Look Samuel, look how high the Holumbe is flying today!"

Samuel shakes his head. "It's Raluvhimba's bird," he mumbles and carries on carefully covering the beans. Anna comes running past again.

"Come Hannes," she calls. "The Holumbe wants to show us something."

I'm tired of gardening and Samuel is taking a long time, so I open the gate and follow them.

"Samuel says the Holumbe is Raluvhimba's bird," I call to Anna, but she doesn't hear me because the Holumbe is flying further and further away from the house. We follow it through the orchard and up past the pine trees behind the church. It won't even let us stop to catch our breath.

"Come, come," it waves and by the time we get to the graveyard, even Asta is panting. We collapse onto the ground. The Holumbe is sitting on a big tree-aloe begging for nectar from sunbird.

Anna and I look at each other. Mutti won't be pleased if she finds out where we are. From up here you can't even see our house. She says that Wilhelmina told her that there are ngangas who walk around in the forest looking for children so they can kill them and use their body parts for medicine. The rest they eat.

It's quiet and peaceful up here. All you can hear is the rustling of the blue gum trees and the bees on the num-nums. There are butterflies everywhere - white and yellow and orange and the big blue ones which sail lazily from flower to flower. We lie back and stare up at the sky. Asta tries to lick my face.

When we were smaller, before Father went to Andalusia, Anna and I used to come up here often on Saturday afternoons with Sarah or Wilhelmina to put flowers on the graves. Anna likes the children's graves best. She says they are sad because they are so small and have angels on them. I like the graves of the two Johannes' because they have the same name as I. Father told me that at the funeral of Evangelist Johannes, Missionary Bester nearly lost his faith. He cried and said, "Why does God take away all the Christians and leave me all alone among the heathens?"

Father said you couldn't really blame Missionary Bester because his first wife and one of her children had died of malaria when they were still living at Old Wittenberg near the river, and then Old Wittenberg was struck by lightning and burnt down and Missionary Bester had to build a whole new mission station up here. Old Wittenberg was built right next to the tshiozwi of the chief because they wanted to show the people that they weren't afraid of the spirits. And now the people believe that Raluvhimba sent the lightning bird to burn down the place.

While Missionary Bester was still building our house, his son from his new wife also died of malaria. He was also Johannes and he was only three months old. They buried him up here so he could be near their new home.

Evangelist Petros died of smallpox. Father told me that Missionary Bester was very cross with him because, even though he told him not to, Evangelist Petros went to the nganga and got medicine to rub all over his sores.

"It's the best way to pass on smallpox," Father told me. "Evangelist Johannes looked after him and then, of course, he also got sick and died."

Later Missionary Bester lost two more children and then his second wife died and he only had a daughter left and he didn't want to stay here anymore so he went back to Germany.

The Holumbe has fallen asleep in the middle of the tree-aloe. Anna is picking some flowers to put on the children's graves. I wish I could go to Andalusia to visit Father. Mutti says the war is getting much worse, they're already bombing Berlin and her sister and our cousins are fleeing into the countryside.

I get up and stretch my arms. Then I make a big big jump. And another one.

"Let's fly to Andalusia."

It's easy, Anna and I just have to jump and jump and jump till we get there.

There is a big fence around the camp but we just jump over it. Father is very happy to see us and we quickly give him mushonga to make him small so we can take him home with us in our pockets. Mutti can't believe what we have done. "You are the best children in the world."

"Let's fly to Berlin," I say. "Then we can fetch Grandmother and Auntie Maria and they can come and live here with us."

So we jump and jump and jump again. We're nearly in Berlin already when Anna stops and puts her hands over her mouth. She rolls her eyes at the graves. "Do you think they can hear us?"

"Who?" I ask.

"The dead people."

For a moment we listen for any noises coming from the graves and then I start to jump again.

Suddenly we hear a rustling in the bushes. We stop. Two children appear, a boy and a girl.

"Who are you?" Anna asks.

You can see that they also got a fright.

"Thambulo wanted to show me the graveyard of the Mufunzi," the girl says shyly.

"We thought you were spirits," Anna says.

The boy is much bigger than me. I've seen him before at Wilhelmina's. I think she's his grandmother.

"Can I see your stick?" the boy asks.

"It's not a stick," I tell him, "it's a sword."

His name is Thambulo. He's from Nshelele and has been at Wittenberg for a few weeks.

"My mukegulu told me that your father is in jail."

I explain that it's not a prison but a camp where they put all the Germans because of the war. And that Adolf Hitler is going to win the war soon and then Father is going to come back home again.

"My father is also gone. He went to Johannesburg to go and work in the mines and he hasn't come back."

"Shame."

The girl is very pretty with big eyes and long legs. Her name is Noria, the daughter of Teacher Lalumbe. She and Thambulo are already in school.

"What about your mother?" Anna asks Thambulo. "Where is she?"

"She went to Johannesburg to look for my father."

Noria steps in front of Thambulo and says to us, "My family is angry with my father."

"Why?" Anna wants to know.

"Because he is a Christian."

Anna and I don't understand

"We can't go home because my father is not talking to them. He doesn't like heathens."

"Your father is very strict," Thambulo teases.

He shows me his stick that he carved with a blade his brother gave him.

Anna shows Noria the children's graves. Noria wants to know if Missionary Bester is our family and Anna tells her that he's from Leipzig and that our family is from Berlin. But not Father's. He's from a village whose name we have forgotten.

"Can you dance tshigombela?" Noria asks Anna.

Anna shakes her head.

"I'll teach you," says Noria. "You just mustn't tell my father. He doesn't want me to do these dances."

Suddenly there is a gust of wind. Noria and Thambulo look at each other. "We have to go now," Thambulo says.

"Why?"

"The spirits don't want us to be here anymore," whispers Noria.

Anna has a good idea. "Why don't you come to our house and we'll show you the Holumbe's garden."

So we march down the hill towards the house together, the Holumbe riding on Asta's back holding tightly onto her hair.

Anna can't stop talking. She tells Noria how the Holumbe made us come to the graveyard today. "Just imagine, he must have known you and Thambulo were coming!"

"You are lucky," says Noria, "you have your own spirit to look after you."

"The Holumbe?" asks Anna. "It just comes and plays with me." So Anna tells Noria about Djambo who is always angry because the hunters shot his family.

"At home in Nshelele I go hunting with my brothers all the time and we bring home meat," says Thambulo.

"Willie is too small to go anywhere with me," I say.

"It's dry there," says Noria. "It's much better here because you can eat as much fruit as you like and there's lots of bush meat also."

"There's much more animals that side," Thambulo argues. "And they're building a big dam."

As soon as we get close to the house we have to speak softly. Mutti doesn't like it if we play with the other children at the mission station.

6.

He was definitely limping much worse than last time. It took him ages to get to the gate to open the padlock. At least there was a tinge of green around the birdbath, it meant that he was still feeding the birds. And the pathetic row of marigolds along the path, always flowering, and the two peach trees that never bore fruit. Mom would have turned this place into an oasis in no time.

Susanna watched her father struggling to open the gate. He was getting thinner and thinner and his back no longer seemed to be able to hold up his tall frame. She should take him to an osteopath, but he would refuse, of course, he hated doctors. Finally he managed to open the gate and she drove in, parking her car in front of the garage. She got out and they hugged stiffly. His body felt light and bony against hers and he smelled of old man.

"Did you get my postcard, Dad?"

A trace of a smile crossed Johannes' face. "Funny, I went to the post office yesterday to go and post a letter to you and there was a post card from you."

"I brought us some delicious things from the city," Susana tried to bubble. "Good coffee, some nice chocolate cookies."

Johannes asked her where her Volkswagen was.

"I've had the 4x4 for two years already, Dad." She wasn't going to get irritated with him. "I even took you for a drive into the koppies with this, last time. Remember?"

Susanna opened the boot and lifted out her large suitcase and bag. Johannes moved to help her but she pointed at the groceries on the back seat.

"Where's Foxy?"

"I had to have him put down."

Her luggage felt heavy this morning and by the time she reached the top of the stairs she was already out of breath. Johannes followed her.

Susanna pushed open the fly screen door with her elbows, the heavy bags blocking her way. The house was hot and stuffy.

"Why don't you open the windows?" she said.

He mumbled something about insects and snakes. Oh God, the old obsessions!

"If you have the fly mesh fixed, you could open all the windows." Susanna emerged from the front room. "I'll pay for it."

"I haven't had time to make your bed and pack everything away," Johannes apologised.

Susanna took the groceries from him and brought them to the kitchen herself.

"I forgot to buy condensed milk." He looked away. "Nowadays I forget things all the time."

"Don't worry." She put on the kettle and started to wipe the kitchen table. The fly paper hanging from the ceiling gave her the creeps, it took the flies so long to stop struggling and dying. The Stillefontein co-op must be one of the last places in the world where you could still buy fly paper.

"How have you been keeping, Dad?"

He looked so frail. As if he could be easily blown over by a gust of wind.

"Why don't you go and sit outside and I'll bring out the coffee. I brought us some fresh bread and mulberry jam from the Stillefontein B&B." She wished he wouldn't hover so.

Finally he shuffled out of the kitchen and onto the veranda. She would have to watch her irritation levels, try to keep calm. At least she had brought her trusty old plunger and they could have endless cups of coffee together. It was a vice they shared.

Susanna took out the tray and cleared the little table next to his chair.

"Look," she said cheerfully. "I found Mom's favourite cups."

She handed him a plate. "What would you think if I came and did some of my PhD research here?"

He didn't respond. She buttered her bread thickly and slopped mulberry jam all over it. She was hungrier than she had thought. The bread was totally delicious.

"Maybe we can do Easter together this year, it must be near your birthday? Aren't you turning 75?"

Johannes shrugged his shoulders. Her phone rang and Susanna

hastily washed down the bread with coffee to answer it.

It was one of her colleagues. Probably wanted to know what had happened in Tanzania so she cut the conversation short. Dad was rocking in his infernal chair, crumbs and mulberry jam all over his shirt.

"The flies are bad here. It's probably to do with the drought cycle."

Johannes nodded.

"Your neighbour should really do something about it at the dairy." Susanna sighed and buttered another slice of bread.

"I always forget how used up everything in this part of the world looks. People just ploughed up the savannah and sent in their cattle to destroy any vestige of the rest." She lit a cigarette and stared into the distance. "The more I find out the more I realise that all that cattle farming is good for is to attract flies."

Johannes continued to rock.

"Have you had any rain this month?"

"23mm."

"Jesus, that's bad. You should get Jooste to chop down those big blue gums, they're huge water guzzlers."

He seemed pre-occupied.

"What's the problem, Dad?"

"There's a woman who makes a fire there at night," he said, pointing at the blue gums. "Keeps me awake. I can hear her. She does things. Singing and praying. Like those prophets we used have walking around Wittenberg."

The way he kept rocking on that chair. The damn thing would break soon. And if not the chair, then the floorboards beneath it. Susanna poured them each another cup of coffee from the plunger and offered Johannes more bread. He shook his head.

"I think I've overdone it a bit over the last few months." She put her feet up on the veranda wall and lit a cigarette. "My boss, Althea, has given me some leave. Do you remember her, I brought her here once? She thinks I might be having a bit of a breakdown."

The bright orange and red wraparound skirt she had bought in Tanzania kept slipping open, so she had to put her legs down again.

"Tanzania's an amazing country, though, Dad. I managed to get away from my conference and organise a driver to take me to an old German mission station. It looked a lot like Wittenberg."

Johannes stopped rocking. The phone rang and Susanna cursed under her breath before answering it.

Johannes got up. "Old man's bladder," he mumbled.

After lunch she lay down on the bed and tried to sleep but it was hot. The front room so full of junk and old papers made her feel even more restless. She should really speak to Dad about getting rid of stuff. Surely he didn't need all these outdated agriculture and forestry journals any more? She could pack them into boxes for him and take them to town for recycling.

Susanna got up and peeped through the curtains. He was still sitting on the veranda, rocking away on his chair. She closed the curtains again. A meadow of flowers - Mom's curtains. She'd bought them on her tour of famous English gardens. Susanna lay down and dozed a bit. Things should be cooling down soon. She felt like going for a long walk up the koppies to clear her head. She hadn't walked up there for a while.

She put on her battle fatigue hiking pants and boots and went into the kitchen to make coffee. It was like an oven in there now, Dad had all the air vents closed in case the snakes came inside. He must have had some bad experiences with snakes in Wittenberg, but whenever she asked him about it he said, "No, the Venda revere snakes."

As she brought the tray with afternoon coffee out onto the veranda, Johannes looked at her anxiously. "Are you going for a walk?"

"Yes. I'll miss taking Foxy with me." She tried to sound cheerful. "Why did you have him put down?"

"He was getting old, incontinent."

Susanna poured the coffee. "When are you going to get another one?"

"Don't want another dog. What will happen to it when I die?"

Susanna got up abruptly to put on sun cream and fill her water bottle with ice water. At least the water was good here. She picked up the big bunch of keys from the breadbin and went back onto the veranda.

"I'm going for my walk now," she said. "Which one is the right key?"

"I never know," Johannes shrugged. "I'll have to come and try them out."

"Don't worry, I'll figure it out." Susanna stopped at the bottom of the stairs. Then trying to soften her tone, "I always forget what that thing was called. The one that you and Auntie Anna used to play with when you were little? The one that made clouds? Your Venda spirit?"

"The Holumbe?"

"The Holumbe, yes! Maybe later you can tell me some Holumbe stories."

It was only after trying almost all the keys that the huge padlock finally snapped open. He must have every single key he has ever owned on this bunch. She wouldn't be surprised if there were keys to Witrivier there.

Susanna strode off towards the koppies through veld strewn with litter. It would take a few years before the land could really recover from a drought like this. Things hadn't looked quite this bad when Dad had first moved here, at least there had been interesting bulbs and a few trees around. But since then Kareepan had expanded.

She missed Foxy. He used to run around like crazy when she took him for a walk, digging in the veld, chasing rats and lizards. He'd been much too brave for his size. Dad should get another dog, he had always had a dog on the farm, walking everywhere with him and driving in the bakkie. Except for Prince. He had been her dog.

Only once she reached the incline towards the koppies did Susanna stop, gasping for air. She lit a cigarette and stared back at the house. Jesus, Dad had really managed to find himself one of the ugliest places possible - the little face brick house squatting blindly over the big bland lawn. The ridiculously high fence that he had insisted on putting up didn't improve things either - with the razor wire on top it looked exactly like an internment camp, all that was missing were some large spotlights and a couple of Alsatians.

Mukegulu tells us a story

Every day Anna and I wait for Noria and Thambulo to finish school so that we can go and play with them, but first we have to make sure that Mutti isn't around. Today she's going to their school to supervise the workers who are building two new classrooms. She wants the classrooms finished before school closes for the December holidays. As soon as she has gone we sneak out of the front door because VhoSarah and Mukegulu Wilhelmina are working in the kitchen and we don't want them to ask lots of questions. From there we go to the church through the Holumbe's garden to meet Noria and Thambulo on the path from the mudi.

The Holumbe is so happy that we have made new friends. Sometimes it turns bright green with joy. Then it looks just like the fresh leaves of the willow tree from which it likes to dangle. Or it buzzes around us, hoping that Noria and Thambulo follow it. It zooms and zips until we are dizzy and Anna has to tell it to go and sit a bit inside Djambo's skull.

Thambulo likes Djambo. He's never seen such a big skull. His mukegulu had told him about the elephant, but he hadn't believed her. She told him that Djambo and his family walked here all the way from Kruger Park. Once, at his home in Nshelele, there was a hippopotamus that attacked people and the villagers had to go and kill it with spears.

"My father was the one who pierced his heart."

"My father can shoot mambas with a gun," I say.

Thambulo tells me that at home he goes hunting in the forest with his friends. They have dogs and they catch birds and rabbits and cook them. At Christmas he is going home again and his brothers are going to take him hunting with real spears.

"I wish I could come with you."

"You mustn't talk about hunting all the time," says Noria pointing at the Holumbe who has gone brown and sulky. "It doesn't like it."

Suddenly the Holumbe flits off into the ink bush with its pink and white trumpets. It picks a flower and drops it onto Anna's head.

"What's it doing?" Noria laughs.

"It's the ink bush," explains Anna. "Mutti says that if you boil the flowers you can make ink and write with it."

We pick a few blossoms and ask Samuel for an old tin and fill it with water. Noria and Anna go to look for a feather to write with while Thambulo and I make a fire. The Holumbe wants to help but it blows so hard that the fire nearly goes out. Once the water boils we add the flowers and it makes a brown mess. But when we try to make marks on the paper, they quickly fade and vanish. Noria suggests that we add more flowers but it doesn't help.

"Let's go swim at the waterfall," Thambulo says.

"I'm not allowed." My heart sinks.

Thambulo looks surprised. "And to Tiger Rock?"

I shake my head. I don't know where Tiger Rock is but Mutti won't let us go anywhere because of the nganga.

"When I was small I also wasn't allowed to go into the forest," Thambulo tries to reassure me.

"But I'm big," I say. "I wish Mutti would let me go to Tiger Rock with you. I want to see the tiger."

On Saturday and Sunday we can't play with Thambulo and Noria because Mutti is at home. All weekend I worry that Thambulo won't want to play with me again because I'm so small and I'm not allowed to go anywhere.

"Why can't I go where I want to?" I ask Mutti.

"Because Hannes, it's dangerous. There are lots of snakes and wild animals out there," Mutti says sternly. "And besides, I need my little man near the house," her voice softens.

"'But if I want to go to Maharaj's?"

Mutti shakes her head.

"And if I go with a friend?"

She ruffles my hair. "Wait till Conrad and Wilfried come to visit."

"But they never take me anywhere. They always say I'm too small."

On Monday it's dip day and many of the boys have to go and help at home, so Teacher Lalumbe has decided to close the school early. Mutti is happy because now the building team can get lots more done.

"Will you be alright eating with Wilhelmina and Sarah?" she asks before she rushes out. Anna and I nod our heads vigorously.

As soon as we can we run off to the church. I'm still a bit worried that Thambulo won't want to play with me again so when I see him coming up the path from Mukegulu's mudi with Noria I'm so relieved that I want to cry.

Anna and Noria run off to practise some tshigombela steps in the Holumbe's garden.

"Maybe we can go to the old mission house today," Thambulo suggests. "VhoSarah says you just have to pray loud enough and the spirits won't do anything to you."

"I'm only allowed to go there with my mother." I want to cry again.

"Don't worry," Thambulo says. "It's very nice here at your house."

I feel terrible. But then I have an idea. "Let's go and play in my room with the Meccano set." I got it from Missionary Els when Father was interned. He told me that Wilfried and Conrad were too old to play with it.

We try to sneak past the girls but it's no use. As soon as Noria and Anna see us they follow us inside. The house is very quiet and Thambulo and Noria are scared. As soon as we get into our room, they sit down on the floor.

I show Thambulo all my things like the cigar box with stamps, and my knife and the toy cars and the building blocks and then we unpack the Meccano set and Thambulo starts building a car. Noria likes our storybooks. She says that we're very lucky to have so many and that not even Teacher Lalumbe has so many.

Suddenly Mutti is standing in the doorway looking angry and pale. The Holumbe gets a big fright and jumps out of the window behind me before Mutti can see it. Noria and Thambulo immediately go on their knees to khotha.

"What are these children doing here?" Mutti asks.

"We're teaching them to read the Bible," I lie.

"Noria and Thambulo are our friends," says Anna.

VhoSarah comes in past Mutti to see what is happening and Thambulo and Noria sit down on the floor behind her.

"This is VhoWilhelmina's grandson, Thambulo," she says. "And

Noria is Teacher Lalumbe's daughter."

Mutti throws us an admonishing look and sighs. "I've got a terrible headache. I won't be surprised if the malaria is starting up again. I don't feel like fighting with you. Just don't play inside the house. It gets dirty easily."

Noria and Thambulo go home immediately and Anna and I spend the rest of the afternoon not knowing what to do with ourselves.

The next day Thambulo suggests that we go and play at his place. I'm sure Mutti won't be happy about it but I can't keep saying that I'm not allowed to do things.

I like Mukegulu Wilhelmina and VhoSarah's mudi. There's a square kitchen hut with a few sleeping huts around it. Even Asta likes it because she can play with Tshamato who has yellow eyes like goat apples.

Thambulo's sister, Masindi, is making food on the fire. She is visiting Mukegulu Wilhelmina with her baby boy. There are two other old ladies there also visiting, and we all go and khotha before them.

"Ndaa."

"Aah," they reply, laughing at Anna and me kneeling in front of them.

Anna and Noria immediately go and pick up the baby and walk around with him. Thambulo and I go and chop wood. At home Mutti never lets me chop wood. She says it's too dangerous.

Finally Mukegulu Wilhelmina arrives and goes to the kitchen hut, rolls out a mat and sits down to relax. A short while later VhoSarah also arrives. She doesn't seem to be cross that we are here.

"I'm so glad you are visiting us, Lufuno," she says to Noria who khothas before her. Anna and I look at her. "But you said your name is Noria?"

Noria looks embarrassed, "That's my Christian name."

We settle down and Masindi serves us stiff porridge and spicy tomato sauce with peanuts on wooden plates. It's delicious.

"Thambulo also has a Christian name," his sister says. "But he doesn't like to use it."

"That's all right." Mukegulu puts her hand on Thambulo's shoulder. "It's good that he is proud of the name his father gave him."

"Even though it means sadness?" Masindi teases.

"I don't want to be called Ezekiel!" Thambulo replies.

"Leave him alone," Mukegulu admonishes. "His name is a gift from his father."

Suddenly there is a loud rumble of thunder. We all look up, surprised. There are no clouds anywhere. Then everybody starts to laugh and clap.

"Raluvhimba!" says Thambulo. "He's coming to talk to the chief."

The adults are smiling.

"Just now Anna and I saw a big eagle fly over the house," Noria says, excited.

"Then it must be Raluvhimba!" Mukegulu's face is shining with happiness.

When we finish eating Asta and Tshamato get to eat the leftovers. We wash the plates in a big enamel bowl and then we all go and sit inside the kitchen hut to rest.

"I'm sure there's enough time for Mukegulu to tell us a story before we have to go back to the kitchen," VhoSarah says as she lies down on a mat and looks at the ceiling.

"But it's still summer," Mukegulu's eyes are twinkling. "If I tell you a story now we are not going to have any crops this year."

"Or maybe you will grow horns," Masindi laughs.

"Please tell us a story, Mukegulu," Noria asks.

"I'm sure Noria never gets to hear a good ngano at home," VhoSarah encourages her. "And the mufunzi's children have probably never even heard of that rascal Sankambe."

"At home no one tells ngano." Noria says.

The adults shake their heads. "Teacher Lalumbe is taking this missionary thing too far," they mutter amongst themselves.

The hut is dark and cool and we wait a bit for the hens to settle onto their nests.

Finally Mukegulu calls out, "Salungano! Salungano! The story begins!"

"Salungano! Salungano!" We call back.

"One day Lion asked Sankambe to look after her ten little cubs," she starts.

"Salungano, Salungano," we repeat. "The story begins."

"As soon as Lion was out of sight the naughty hare decided that he was a bit hungry so he ate one of the cubs. When Lion came home that night she asked Sankambe. 'Is everything fine? Are all my children well?'

And the hare replied, 'Of course Lion, all your children are fine. Look here!' And Sankambe picked up each cub and counted: 'One, two, three, four, five,' he counted and when he got to the last cub he lifted it up twice and counted - 'nine, ten.'

The lioness was satisfied and the next day Sankambe came and looked after the cubs again. And again, as soon as mother Lion had gone the little rascal ate another of the cubs.

That night when Lion came home from the hunt she asked again: 'Are all my cubs fine, Sankambe?'

And Sankambe said, 'Yes, they are all fine.' And then he counted the cubs again. 'One, two, three, four, five, six, seven.' And when he came to the eighth cub, Sankambe lifted it up three times and counted: 'Eight, nine, and ten.'

The next day Sankambe ate another cub and the day after that another one, and so on, until there was only one cub left.

That night when the lioness came home she asked Sankambe again, 'Are all my cubs fine, Sankambe? Did you look after them well?'

Sankambe replied, 'Yes, they are fine.' He lifted the last cub ten times and counted 'One, two, three, four, five, six, seven, eight, nine, ten.' And then the hare went home.

The next day Sankambe ate the last cub. But now he was a little worried.

'Oh, oh, what shall I say to the lioness when she comes home?' And then he had an idea. He went into the bush and rolled himself in the dust and in the mud. Then he took some thorns and scratched himself all over.

When Lion came home, Sankambe greeted her with moans and groans. 'Look, look what the baboons have done. They came and ate up all your cubs' he said. 'And I couldn't protect them.' He held his head and started to cry.

The lioness was furious. She paced up and down. 'I'm going to go and kill all those baboons, she growled. 'Let's go Sankambe, let's go and take revenge.'

The little rascal sat up and dried his tears, 'I agree, Lion, we must retaliate,' he said. 'But I want to suggest something.'

'What do you suggest?' she roared.

'If the baboons see you arriving with me they will all run away because they will know why you have come and we won't be able to get our revenge. No,' the hare said earnestly, 'we have to catch them by surprise. You have to climb into this sack and then, once we get there you can jump out and surprise them.'

So Sankambe and Lion went to see the baboons and just before they got there the lioness climbed into the sack and Sankambe carried her.

'Hullo,' Sankambe put down his heavy sack and greeted the baboons. While they were still exchanging pleasantries a baby baboon that was clinging onto its mother's back pointed at the sack and said. 'Look Mommy look, there are some green eyes shining in that sack.'

'You are mistaken little one,' Sankambe said quickly and continued his conversation with the adults. After a while the little baboon pointed at the sack again: 'But look, there they are – there are eyes gleaming in that bag.'

Just then the lioness jumped out and attacked the baboons, roaring with anger. All you could hear was bones breaking and fur flying. It was an almighty battle.

And Sankambe? As soon as the fighting started the little villain ran off into the night feeling mighty pleased with himself for having tricked Lion."

7

Mom's garden in Witrivier was magical. There was the herb garden with a narrow curving path that forced you to brush up against the aromatic bushes and surprised you with poppies and strawberries and giant nettles. The big pond she created after Granddad Maclear had died had a bench where you could sit and stare at the Japanese fighting fish, the water lilies and the dark purple water irises, and wait for the white herons to come and wade amongst the rushes and ferns. Then there was the little rose garden with the fountain and the grassland garden, swaying richly in the wind.

Dad never gave her a cent. He always resisted everything she wanted to do or change. Only when Granddad Maclear died and left her some money, did Mom manage to go and buy gardening books and plants to her hearts content. She would drive all the way to Pretoria to get to the best nurseries. She had loved going with Mom and sometimes, after the nurseries, they went to visit Auntie Anna.

One year Mom even went with a garden club on a tour of gardens in England. Susanna had never seen her so alive. She had even let her usually tightly cropped grey hair grow a little longer and had sewn herself three new dresses for the trip with old fashioned floral materials she had been saving for years. The tight waist and flared skirts made her tiny frame look girlish and happy.

And all the way from the airport back to Witrivier Mom just couldn't stop talking. She described each garden she had seen in the most vivid details, speaking with disdain of the overly cultivated and formal Italian ones and with obvious relish about the wild gardens that spilled over into the landscape.

"I'm ready to die now!" She glowed. "I've got a good idea what the Garden of Eden looks like."

When they got home Dad seemed even more withdrawn than usual. But Mom didn't even notice. All she wanted to do was to get back to her garden and the grasslands around the plantations to collect seeds, bulbs and grasses.

They used to get on so well, Mom and her. Even when she was small she used to help Mom in the garden – cutting dead flowers or collecting snails in a bucket and pouring salt onto them. When she had had enough, she would climb up the avocado tree and surprise whoever was walking below by throwing pebbles down on them. Or she would spend hours watching the fish in the pond, feeding them Quaker Oats.

Then Prince arrived. It was her last year before she went to boarding school. Dad brought him home one day, a half Alsatian, emaciated and skittish. He never told them where he had found Prince, but it didn't matter, he was a beautiful dog. Susanna had been going on and on to Dad about buying her a horse, because all the girls at school had horses, but he wasn't budging.

"Horses aren't toys, Susanna," he used to say sternly.

She called her dog Prince, like a horse she had read about, and started training him. She went to the municipal library and took out every book she could get hold of on dogs and how to train them. Mom bought her more for her birthday. She set up an obstacle course on the lower lawn using old drums and tyres and ropes. Prince and she spent every spare minute in the garden together. He would jump through tyres, run up steep inclines and balance on top of planks.

Then Dad would come home from the plantations for lunch or in the early evening after work and spoil everything. When she heard the sound of his bakkie driving through the plantations, Susanna's heart would sink. He always seemed to be in a bad mood or just miserable, getting out of the bakkie without greeting them and immediately withdrawing into his study. At mealtimes he somehow managed to completely dry up any conversations. Every evening, she couldn't wait for him to go and hide himself again in that musty room with his journals and graphs.

As soon as the heavy door closed she and Mom would call Prince inside so that he could come and lie with them on the ugly old Berlin sofa in the lounge. In winter they would play cards or read. Sometimes they lit the lamps from Wittenberg and Mom would tell her stories about the adventures of Great Grandfather Maclear who was a trader in a far-off outpost of Lesotho. And about Grandma Maclear who was soft and fey and used to sing so beautifully in church that it would make people cry. Mom told her how her father had refused to let her study botany because he felt it wasn't right for girls to go to university and, besides, he needed someone to stay on the farm with him after Grandma died. Mom used to smile at Susanna's angry reaction to this.

"Don't worry, Susanna," she would say. "Now I've got you and my garden."

"And Dad," Susanna would add in a bitter voice.

"You mustn't be so harsh on him." Mom tried to soothe her. "He's just a quiet man. He didn't have it easy as a child."

As Susanna got older things between her and Dad got worse. One year, it must have been when she was in Standard 8, she made the mistake of bringing one of her school friends home with her for the holidays. Maureen was tall and pretty and came from Johannesburg where her father was a lawyer who specialised in defending anti-apartheid activists. Her parents were rich and they had sent her specifically to Swaziland so that she could attend a multiracial school. Maureen and Susanna hadn't been friends immediately, but when they both got through to the debating national finals in Johannesburg, Susanna stayed with Maureen's family. She'd never seen such a lovely house before; it was full of paintings by young black artists and even had a grand piano in the large modern lounge. Her father was tall and charming and her mother had a mane of black hair that made her look like an opera singer.

Then it was Maureen's turn to visit them. Susanna had been nervous - their house was small and dull compared to Maureen's and she was embarrassed by Dad's sullenness and Mom's plainness. She could immediately see that her friend was disappointed there were no horses on the farm, but she managed to impress her by showing her all the tricks that Prince could do.

On the second day they went for a long long walk through the plantations, talking endlessly, occasionally resting under a big tree. Susanna told her how much she hated Dad with all his weird habits and his clumsy German English that sounded like he was Afrikaans.

"And we never get to go anywhere. Dad always says that we can't leave because there is no one to look after the farm."

Maureen told her that her dad was a member of the South African Communist party and that she was scared that the police were going to come and take him away.

"That's why I have to go to school in Swaziland."

Susanna felt mortified. Her problems seemed so much less grand compared to Maureen's. She had never met someone who secretly belonged to the Communist Party before. When they got home from the walk and Maureen was in the dining room phoning her parents, Susanna told her mother that she thought that she had finally found a friend.

As usual Dad came home late that night, barely greeting them and hastening to lock himself up in his study. Susanna couldn't help noticing how shabby he looked, how uncomfortable he made Maureen feel and she remembered Maureen's father with his dinner-time conversation, attentive and charmingly curious about Susanna's political leanings and views.

The next evening after Dad had locked himself up in his study again, Maureen asked if he was always like this.

"Like what?"

"Like he doesn't like me?"

"Of course he likes you."

"Do you think he wants me to go?"

Susanna didn't know what to say.

Maureen nodded towards his study. "What does he do in there all the time?"

Susanna shrugged, "I really don't know. I think he reads. Farming journals, books."

"All night long?"

Susanna was getting more unsure of herself now.

The next day she asked Mom to speak to Dad, but it didn't help. As the week progressed it became more and more uncomfortable and it was almost a relief when they finally took Maureen to the station on Friday.

"Why was Dad so terrible to Maureen?" Susanna demanded to know as they got back into the bakkie.

"He's shy with strangers," Mom said. "It's from growing up on a mission station."

"No. He's just plain weird." Tears were running down her face now. "Even Maureen says so."

Mom didn't say anything.

"And I won't be surprised if she doesn't want to be my friend anymore next term."

"He's not a bad man, your father."

"I hate him. And I'm never ever going to bring a friend home again."

When they had finished their shopping at the co-op, they drove back to the farm in silence. All the way Susanna planned how she would punish Dad by ignoring him for the rest of the holidays. But when they got home and saw what he had done to Prince, she knew she would never forgive him.

A **bad** day

Mutti is in a very bad mood. The Malombo women have been drumming and singing for three days and nights already. VhoSarah told us that there's a woman in the mudi near Maharaj's who's possessed and now the Malombos have come to heal her. Mutti says they'll just fill her with lots of superstitious nonsense and that Sarah and Wilhelmina should at least have told her that someone was sick. Then she could go and see what's going on and call a doctor or pray for her. Now Mutti hasn't slept for the last three nights.

"And that isn't good for my health,''' she says as she cleans the kitchen.

But I don't care. I'm so angry with Mutti. This morning she told Samuel to tie Asta to the frangipani tree because Asta has been stealing eggs from the chickens' nests.

"It's not fair," I tell her. "Asta only has three legs and now you're tying her up as well."

"The rope is long enough for her to move around," Mutti snaps at me.

It was Missionary Els who suggested it. He told Mutti to force Asta to eat an egg full of chilli powder. She even made me go to Maharaja's to buy it, all alone.

"You'll see Elisabeth. That dog of yours will never steal an egg again," Missionary Els laughed.

It didn't work and now Asta is tied up and howling and whining outside.

"Can't we get rid of the chicken?" I want to kill something.

"Young man," Mutti says, "where do you think we're going to get eggs and meat from? In case you've forgotten, there's a war going on in Europe and we're lucky still to be getting half your father's salary. Uncle Els told me that most of the Natal missionaries haven't had a salary from Germany for months already." Everything she sees in the kitchen gets wiped with her cloth. "We can only expect things to get worse. Germany has to put all its resources into the war effort now. They can't pay us much longer." She can't seem to stop cleaning. "Just the other day Uncle Els was saying that we all have to become more self-sufficient."

I hate Uncle Els, he always knows everything better. "Mukegulu Wilhelmina lets her chickens stay inside the house."

"That brings me onto something else, young man. "I already regret that I said anything. " This place is becoming a pig sty," Mutti interrupts herself. Then she continues. "Don't think that I haven't noticed that you've been spending afternoons at Wilhelmina's house."

"Thambulo and I are helping Mukegulu with her garden.,"

Asta starts to howl again. I want to go outside and console her.

"There's quite enough for you to do here, thank you." Now she is taking down all the preserves and wiping their lids. "And you and Anna are speaking too much Tshivenda anyhow."

Just then Anna walks into the kitchen. She's on her way out to visit Noria who's got a new baby brother.

Mutti stops her. "That goes for you too, young lady, all this going outside whenever you feel like it has to stop." Anna looks at her, surprised.

"And go and put on some decent clothes," Mutti rips the tablecloth off the kitchen table and shakes it. "My children are turning into little barbarians right in front of my own eyes." She starts to scrub the kitchen table. "When you're dressed properly, you can come back and help me."

Anna goes back to her room and Mutti mutters, "I just wish someone would stop that infernal drumming."

When I finally manage to slip out of the kitchen I go and sit with Asta under the frangipani tree. She immediately stops howling and sits close against me, shivering.

"One day I am going to have my own house," I promise her. "And then you can eat as many eggs as you like."

Asta sighs, curls up next to me and falls asleep, but after a while I don't feel like sitting there in the dust anymore so I go to look for Anna who has finished helping Mutti. I find her in the Holumbe's garden. I can see that she's angry because she's not allowed to visit Noria. I start throwing little grains of sand into the flesh eaters.

Anna turns on me. "Don't do that, you'll kill them."

I laugh at her and then the Holumbe comes and glares at me and I glare back and I start throwing sand at it.

I want to see it cry.

"Stop that Hannes!" shouts Anna. "You're going to kill the Holumbe!"

"It won't die from a bit of sand."

"It will, it will!" Anna stomps her foot, "Spirits die easily. Mukegulu told me."

"The Holumbe is not a spirit."

"Then what is it?"

"Just a stupid thing that cries easily, like you."

The Holumbe makes angry green sparks at me and I stick out my tongue at it.

"It must die. It's a stupid thing."

Anna is close to tears now. "You're so mean!" She walks off.

I throw sand after her and watch her run up along the path past the church to the forest.

"You're not allowed to go into the forest," I shout after her.

Anna vanishes and Asta whines and strains against the rope again. I throw a pine cone at her and she wags her tail. Now I feel bad and go to untie the rope. I don't care what Mutti says. Asta is happy and we walk along the path following Anna. When we get to the church I climb up the embankment and sit under a big pine tree. The drumming is much louder here. The ground is covered with prickly pine needles and I find a smelly red mushroom full of flies and cut it open with my penknife and look inside.

A bit later I see Anna coming back on the path on the other side of the church. She looks so small.

"Come, see what I found," I call.

At first she ignores me. But when I call her again she turns around and comes closer. "We can go and play in the treehouse."

She smiles and slowly comes up the embankment to join me. Her feet slip on the pine needles. I can see that she's been crying.

I look for something in my pocket and find the shell that Sixpence gave me. Sixpence is one of the prophets who always comes to ask for a sixpence at the kitchen door. He told me the shell can make you hear things from far away, but it doesn't really work. All I can hear is the drumming.

"Here, you can have this," I give Anna the shell and show her the smelly mushroom. She wrinkles her nose and smiles. We lie back on the thick bed of pine needles and watch the clouds, the dragons and rabbits flying through the air and then we see the map of England and the Holumbe comes to join us. It starts to make clouds with its bum and we laugh a lot.

Suddenly the drumming stops.

"The bad spirit has left the woman," whispers Anna.

We lie back and look at the clouds some more. The sun is shining but heavy glittering drops of rain fall on us through the pine trees. When it rains harder we get up and run back to the house with the Holumbe riding on Asta's back.

As soon as we get to the veranda I tie Asta up again. But Mutti isn't cross. There's a letter from Father lying on the kitchen table.

"I'm going to make us sausages and Bratkartoffeln for lunch," Mutti says cheerfully. "I found a bottle of sauerkraut in the pantry that is ready to explode."

But first she folds open Father's letter and composes herself.

"Your Father says that you shouldn't be spending so much time with the local children otherwise your German will suffer."

Anna and I keep quiet.

"And just imagine, he's managed to take time off from his studies to write a story for the two of you!"

We sit down and Mutti clears her throat and reads:

Once upon a time there was a boy called Peter. He was very, very naughty and never listened to his mother. His father was a soldier who had gone to war and his poor mother cried a lot. But Peter didn't care. All he wanted to do was play all day long.
One day his mother had gone off into the forest to go and fetch wood when a soldier appeared in the yard. He had lost one leg in the war and he was on crutches. He asked the boy: 'Won't you fetch me some water from your well?'
The boy was so busy playing that he said: 'Why don't you go and fetch your own water?'
And the man said, 'Because I can't, I have lost my leg in the war.'
The boy ignored the soldier and carried on playing. He didn't notice

that the soldier was very angry and that he went back into the forest to look for the mother of this rude boy. No, the boy just carried on playing till it was dark and he grew hungry.

'I wonder when mother is coming back home to cook?' he said to himself.

And he waited and waited for his mother to come back from the forest to make him some food, and he became very cold and scared.

'What if I get attacked by a wolf?' he cried and crept into his mother's house. The whole night he lay shaking and shivering and crying. And he thought about his mother and how he had never listened to her and about how much she had done for him and how he had never helped her.

The night was long and dark and the boy only fell asleep when it was early morning. And when he woke up the sun was already very high and he could smell some porridge cooking. He jumped out of his bed and there was his mother standing in the kitchen cooking. He was overcome with joy. And next to her was the soldier with one leg. It was his father who had come back from the war.

And from that day on Peter always helped his mother with everything.

We sit quietly for a while, then suddenly Anna says, "That is a stupid story!"

Mutti drops the letter on the kitchen table. "How dare you, Anna!"

"What if the wolf had come and eaten Peter in the night? What then?"

"Your father wrote that story for you," Mutti is very angry.

And then, as if the devil has got hold of her, Anna laughs out loud. "The parents would have been very sorry if that happened, I mean if the wolf had eaten Peter."

Mutti goes pale and slaps Anna across the face. "Go to your beds immediately, you ungrateful children."

I rush off after Anna and we lie down on our beds. It's strange because it's only lunch time and the room is very bright and we haven't even washed yet.

Anna and I lie quietly for a long time and, just as I'm about to scold her for getting us into trouble, I hear Mutti's footsteps outside our door. Then we must have fallen asleep because later when Mutti comes with a tray with cold Bratkartoffeln and sauerkraut and sausages, it's already dark outside.

"I want the two of you to eat your supper now and then brush your teeth and put on your pyjamas." Her voice is still angry. "Hannes, you can come and say goodnight to me."

When I finish brushing my teeth I walk down the passage to her bedroom.

Mutti is lying on the big bed. "Come and lie next to me," she says sweetly. "You know that I love you both very much?"

She strokes my hair and I relax against her. "I just feel so alone without your father sometimes."

I don't say anything.

"I have thought about Asta stealing the eggs," Mutti says softly. "There's that storeroom next to Father's study that no one is using at the moment. Maybe we could let the chickens lay their eggs in there. Just leave the window open for them to get in and out and then we can let Asta go free again. What do you think?"

I jump up to go and tell Anna, but Mutti pulls me back. "Not so fast young man," she laughs and kisses me on the forehead.

When I get to our room Anna comes and lies next to me on the bed and I tell her that Asta will be free again.

"I am a bit scared," she says.

"Anna, you must tell Mutti that you're sorry for laughing at the story. What if she dies? Or if the police come and take her to the camp in Salisbury?"

Anna promises she'll be nice to Mutti. The moon rises in the window. There's an Eagle Owl hooting in the trees and we fall asleep.

8.

Now that the sun was lowering itself into the West it was getting a bit cooler. Johannes held up his binoculars and watched the dried-up hills in the distance. The tin roof crackled from the contraction. It was a relief to have Susanna out of the house for a bit - always organising and telling him what he should do. But now she had been away for almost two hours and he was getting worried.

She'd looked like a game ranger in her khaki pants and boots, striding off into the veld with her short strong legs and unruly hair tucked under a cap. Even as a small child Susanna had loved walking through the plantations, skipping next to him, asking questions. That was before she went off to boarding school in Swaziland. She had insisted on going to that expensive school, said she wanted to be with her friends and ride horses. Then in the holidays she had come home and ignored him.

She'd always preferred Kate's company. Had her wrapped around her little finger. Constantly scheming how she could get things out of him through Kate – a bicycle, a horse. She had been relentless about getting a horse. Maybe he'd been a bit stubborn about it. At least he could have taken them on holidays sometimes, Kate and Susanna, to the sea or the game park. But he hated holidays. All the fuss and the packing and the people everywhere. What for? He was much happier at home studying his journals. Father had never taken them on holidays either, he hadn't had time for such frivolities.

Johannes got up from his rocking chair, wondering if he should start cooking their supper. The sun would be setting just now and then the mosquitoes would come out. On his way to the kitchen, he turned on the veranda light, just in case she was lost.

The pantry cupboard was full of things she had brought and even the fridge seemed overflowing. She had probably already planned what they would eat tonight. Her phone rang and Johannes went to the front room to go and look for it. The veranda light shone through the flowery curtains. She had kept the curtains closed.

Such an untidy girl, her things lying about everywhere. The ringing came from out of one of her bags - a Bach fugue. It sounded so insistent. Johannes hesitated before he gingerly pushed his hand into the large bag filled with clothes. Then it stopped. He was relieved. Maybe he should go and bath now so that there would be enough hot water when she came back. She liked to use lots of water in her bath. He would put on a fresh shirt and maybe they could sit in the lounge and light the lamps tonight. She enjoyed that.

He went into the lounge to check that the lamps had enough paraffin in them. As he lifted each lamp he could feel Mutti and Father's gaze on him from their picture on the wall. The room smelled of paraffin. The light on the veranda cast a thick ray through the gap in the curtains and the Berlin furniture looked even larger and more sombre than usual. Kate had hated it. "It looks so unkind," she had said when she first saw it.

"You'll get used to it."

By now all the lamps would have been lit in Wittenberg and they would have gathered around the large kitchen table - VhoSarah, Mukegulu Wilhelmina, Anna, Mutti, Willie and he. Everything would be quiet as they waited for Mutti to find a passage from the Bible to read to them. Those strange musical words so precious to her – sometimes harsh and at other times filled with the longing of ages. Sometimes Mutti would get lost in her prayers. She would pray for Father in the camp; for their relatives in Germany whose names were familiar but whom they had never met; and for all the souls in Venda that had not found God yet. Once she carried on praying so long that Anna started to make irreverent shadows on the wall with her hands and he had to try everything to stop himself from laughing out loud.

And then the hymns. *'Oh, stay with us for it is night'* was Mutti's favourite. Her voice had been sweet and high like a child's. Anna also had a clear voice. He would harmonise with VhoSarah and Mukegulu who took turns to beat the rhythm cushion.

Johannes wiped his face. Silly old man! Carrying his bladder between his eyes.

The bath always took such a long time to fill and Johannes went out once more onto the veranda to survey the koppies. She was nowhere to be seen. Slowly he moved the binoculars over to the car wreck - there was no one there either. It was a pity that Foxy wasn't there to walk with her. Johannes put down the binoculars and quickly went back into the house. Had to stop all this thinking, the bath was probably running over already.

At first he couldn't find his towel and then he discovered it hidden under Susanna's huge red one which filled the whole rail. Johannes took off his clothes and carefully stepped into the bath. It was good to float in the water, he should do it more often. Normally he just used a face cloth to wash himself in the basin - a catwash Mutti had called it. Didn't really like to take off his clothes. His body so thin and worn. Blue veins worming their way across his skin. Sunken chest. In the early months of their marriage he and Kate had sometimes bathed together. Her body was always compact, her breasts small and firm. But after Susanna's birth he hadn't seen her naked much. She had been such a good woman, his Kate. Kind and gentle, she seldom got cross. He had never understood why she had to go and die so suddenly, just as they were going to move here. Maybe they would have had the chance to get to know each other again, talk and go for walks together. It was strange how she died like that. But things had always been like that with her – strange somehow. Even the way they had met.

He had been working for the Mission Society as a farm manager for seven years already when the Society was dissolved. He had never thought that he would have to go and look for work somewhere else, but luckily he saw an advertisement for a farm manager in the Farmer's Weekly. When he called the number Mr Maclear didn't seem too keen to employ a German, yet when he discovered that Johannes had been to agricultural college with his two sons, Mr Maclear took him on probation for a few months to see how they would get along. Johannes immediately felt at home on Witrivier. The farm was surrounded by gentle mountains and lush grasslands and Mr Maclear and he somehow managed to work well together. He had noticed her immediately - Mr Maclear's daughter, Kate. She struck him as someone who enjoyed her own company - a quiet girl who got on with life. Small with mousy short hair and kind eyes.

It took him six months to muster enough courage to ask her to go for a walk with him, and then they got into the habit of going for walks on Saturday afternoons. They spoke about plants and trees, sometimes about their lives. And then, one afternoon, after she had left him at the door of his cottage he had suddenly panicked, painfully, that he wouldn't be able to live without her.

On their next walk he asked her to marry him and was surprised when she accepted him. They were walking by a stream in one of the last pieces of natural forest on the farm and when she had told him that it was her favourite place, he had said that it reminded him of the forests around Wittenberg. He didn't even kiss her when she said that she would marry him, didn't know how to. They just held hands for a short while. Her hands were strong, those of a practical person.

Later, when the price of paper had gone up, he had had that piece of forest chopped down to extend the pine plantations and Kate didn't talk to him for days. It was one of the few times ever that he saw her really angry. That, and when he bought this house here at Stillefontein. Susanna still resented him for buying the house. Once, during one of their fights, she had told him that Kate died because she didn't want to move here.

"She just gave up trying to make you listen to what she needed, Dad!" They had always fought ugly, he and Susanna.

"You killed her Dad," she had said. "Like you kill everything else around you."

She never forgave him for shooting Prince. He had told her over and over again that the dog was foaming at the mouth and that Franz Muller had shot a rabid rabbit only a few days previously.

Johannes immersed his head under the water. Maybe he could just stay there for a while, maybe forever, just vanish into the water. He had wanted to spare her. After a while he came up for breath again. Wasn't a good idea to be discovered dead in the bath by Susanna, and, knowing her, she would just be angry with him again.

When he had asked Kate's father for permission to marry her, Mr Maclear had hesitated. His wife had died a few years before and Kate was his only daughter. He called Kate into his office. Johannes never found out what they said to each other but they came out about half an hour later, smiling, and Mr Maclear had wished them well and poured himself and Johannes a stiff whiskey. He had never drunk whiskey before and thought it tasted terrible.

Father, on the other hand, had been furious. Asked him sternly how he intended to bring up his children in the Lutheran faith if the mother was a Methodist. Johannes had shrugged his shoulders. Then Father asked what language he planned to speak to his children.

"English," Johannes had replied. Father shook his head disapprovingly. At least Willie had married a nice German girl, he said.

Father and Mutti drove to their wedding all the way from the Lutheran old age home in Pretoria and then left again soon after the church service. Didn't even stay for the reception.

They had been happy together in the early days, he and Kate. Every afternoon they had taken the dogs for long walks all over the farm. Then after three years, Susanna arrived – a screaming, angry, red little thing. At first Kate had tried to include him, asked him to hold the baby, help with the feeding. But he just couldn't do it. It was as if the little thing disliked him right from the beginning. As soon as he tried to pick her up, she screamed at the top of her voice and Kate soon moved out of their bedroom to be with the infant at night.

From when she was small, Susanna had made it quite clear that she didn't need him. She was happy just to be with Kate. They worked in the garden together, drove to Piet Retief to do the shopping, told each other stories and laughed. Maybe he had withdrawn too quickly, given up too easily, but by the time Susanna left home to go to boarding school, it was too late already. Kate threw all her energy into the garden, while he carried on farming as if nothing had changed.

Johannes sighed and got out of the bath and dried himself. He started to worry again. What if something had happened to Susanna? Stumbled over a puffadder or something?

It was almost completely dark by the time he walked out onto the veranda again. His hair was still wet and the new shirt chafed his neck. He couldn't see much, just the faint pale rim of the sky in the west over the blackened earth. Maybe the rains would never come back again.

We start school

After Christmas the rains stop and it gets hot and dry. Mutti says we're going to have to start praying for rain in church soon because it will be a disaster if the maize crop fails.

"The heathens will find some way to blame us."

One morning she calls Anna and me into the kitchen and announces that it's time that we go to school. She's going to turn the visitor's lounge into a schoolroom, she says, and be our teacher.

"But we want to go to proper school with the other children," I say.

"Anna is only five, they won't accept her," Mutti replies.

"I'm going to be six in November," Anna protests. "And Hannes is going to be seven at Easter and he lost his front teeth already and Uncle Els says that it means that he is ready to go to big school with Conrad and Wilfried."

I wish Anna would keep quiet and stop getting us deeper into trouble.

"I refuse to send my children to boarding school while their father is sitting in an internment camp."

"But why can't we go to school with Thambulo and Noria, with Teacher Lalumbe?"

Mutti looks at us. "In case you have forgotten I am a trained teacher. And you can't go to the mission school."

"Why not?"

"It's not for you."

"Why?"

"It's for African children." Mutti is obviously disappointed by our reaction.

"Why?" But Anna knows she is already defeated and Mutti marches off to the lounge and noisily moves the big Berlin sofa and armchairs into a corner.

Soon Teacher Lalumbe arranges for two desks to be brought to our new schoolroom and Mutti turns the small kitchen table into a teacher's desk. She has also managed to get a large blackboard on a stand from somewhere.

Every night she sits in the schoolroom till late, the lamps burning, making readers for us - cutting pictures out of old magazines and Mission Society newsletters and writing sentences underneath them.

"I wish I had brought more textbooks with me from Germany," she says.

The day before school starts, a letter arrives from Father. Mutti says that he agrees that we aren't allowed to go to mission school with Thambulo and Noria.

"What if we promise to speak only German to each other?" Anna doesn't give up easily. "Can we go to the mission school then?"

I kick Anna under the table but she doesn't seem to notice.

"I don't want to talk about this anymore," Mutti says.

After a long silence she picks up the letter again and smiles forcefully: "Father says that Christmas at Andalusia was lovely. The men's choir had rehearsed all the carols and they even decorated a thorn tree like a Christmas tree. The Red Cross donated extra sugar and spices and the bakers made lovely Christmas cookies. Even the warders said they were much better than the English ones they had at home."

"Is Father a Nazi?" Anna asks.

"You silly child," Mutti laughs. "Why do you ask such a thing?"

"Wilfried told me that he wants to be a Nazi when he grows up."

"No." Mutti is serious again. "Your father is a man of God."

Later that day Missionary Els fetches Mutti in his car so that she can get a few more things in Louis Trichardt for our school. As soon as they are gone, Anna and I run to fetch Noria and Thambulo who are still on holiday to show them our new schoolroom. They look at the big map of Europe that Mutti has hung up and I show Thambulo the places Hitler has already invaded.

Thambulo and I decide to go outside and play war, but the girls don't want to join us. They're playing a girl's game about making rain because Noria has a friend in school who is from Tzaneen and she told her about Modjaji. She's the queen of the Lovedu and Noria's friend has seen her.

"A real rain queen?" Anna is awed.

Thambulo says that Mukegulu told him that when there is a drought, it is Raluvhimba who is punishing us and someone has to go to the Matopo Mountains and offer him a black ox.

"There are people in Nshelele who know how to make rain," he adds.

"But Modjaji is a real queen," Anna says.

We leave them to it and play war. Thambulo and I are the Germans! We throw bombs on Britain and on London. When I want to throw bombs on Johannesburg because South Africa is part of Britain, Thambulo says that maybe we shouldn't do that because his father and mother and brother are all living there. The Holumbe sits in the tree looking purple and making ugly faces with long teeth.

Then Thambulo and I have a good idea. We fill banana leaves with water and start to throw them at the girls. "Rainbombs, rainbombs from Modjaji!"

The girls are cross and Anna declares that they are going to fight in the war against us.

"You have to be England then," I tell them.

"That's fine!" says Noria. "My father says Churchill is a great leader."

Germans have better airpower than Britain, so Thambulo and I attack from the sky. Anna says they are going to use giant birds to attack us. The Holumbe tries to make loud noises like an aeroplane but it doesn't quite manage.

Suddenly it starts to rain and we have to run onto the little veranda at the front door. Red and green lightning shoots through the clouds and the rain beats down noisily on the tin roof. Then the hail starts. The girls huddle together.

"Anna?" Noria looks frightened. "Do you think we made rain?" They hold their hands in front of their mouths and start to laugh.

The Holumbe is dancing around under the tree, imitating the girls' rain dance, grinning. Then it sees Anna's doll Ella lying naked in the rain, the mud on her body washing off. It goes and sits next to her trying to protect her. Noria runs out into the downpour to fetch Ella.

"See, Modjaji is stronger than Germany," she says breathlessly as she joins us under the veranda again. Her hair is completely wet and her eyes are shining. It is hailing harder and we can't hear anything anymore except the drumming of the hail on the roof. Now the Holumbe also joins us on the veranda, sitting inside Djambo's skull. The large white hailstones are hitting everything in sight – leaves and flowers are shredded.

The next day Thambulo and Noria go to their school and we begin lessons with Mutti. Anna refuses to put on the school shoes with laces that Mutti bought for her in Louis Trichardt. She doesn't like to wear shoes. She says they hurt her.

"We aren't going to a real school," she argues, pointing at the sofa and the big clock in the schoolroom. "Why do I have to wear these horrible shoes?"

"Of course this is a real school," Mutti says. "We are going to have a timetable and a real bell, and you are going to behave yourself."

During the first lesson Mutti reads us a story from the Bible. The big clock ticks all the time. Then we look at the map and learn the names of all the countries around Germany and afterwards we practise making shapes on our slates. When the clock strikes ten times, Mutti rings the bell, Sarah brings us milk and ginger biscuits and then we're allowed to go and play outside for a bit.

We run to the Holumbe's garden, which is littered with flowers from yesterday's hail. Anna says it looks like there's been a wedding and I say it looks more like after a battle and we laugh and by the time the bell rings again, we have played with the Holumbe and forgotten all the names of the countries around Germany.

9.

Just as his eyes were adjusting to the dark, the gate squeaked open and Susanna came striding up the stairs towards him. Her hair had been released from the cap and her face looked flushed and happy.

"Look Dad," she said and she held out a bunch of veld flowers and grasses towards him. "I found these red crassulas near the sweet-thorn grove on the south side of the koppies where we went walking with Foxy that one time."

She smiled at him. "I had such a wonderful walk. Saw two buck - mountain rheebuck!" She was out of breath. "It's pretty up there. I want to find out if the area's been declared a conservancy. It would be a pity if it hasn't. Those iron age walls are wonderful."

He wanted to go inside but instead he turned towards her. "It was terrible, the thing with Foxy." His voice was thin and dry. "When the vet gave him the injection, you know, the one to put him down, he sat up and looked me straight in the eyes."

Susanna walked past him and into her room. He shrank from her touch.

"What do you say I make us some food, Dad?" He could hear her sit down on the bed, her boots thudding onto the floor.

"I'll put on the oven and get the pasta sauce ready," she said. "And then I'll have a quick bath."

He would let her get on with things, sit in his room for a bit.

When he heard her come out of the bathroom again, Johannes quickly went into the kitchen to set the table.

"It's much too hot to eat in here, Dad."

Susanna smelled of soap and shampoo. He tried to protest about the mosquitoes and the snakes, but she just carried everything out onto the veranda and put it down on the rickety little folding table that she had covered with a tablecloth. It was the one with the red poppies that Kate had brought back from her trip to England. It always baffled him how Susanna managed to find things in his house, things he had completely forgotten about.

The moon was rising in the east. It must have been full moon yesterday. He could hear her rummaging around in the lounge now. What was she up to?

"Let's sit in here while we wait for the pasta to cook, Dad. It'll only be another thirty minutes."

Johannes got up wearily from his chair. He felt like coffee. He found her busy lighting the brass lamps, placing them on the sideboard and coffee table. A wallspider scuttled out from behind Elisabeth and Wilhelm Weber. She had placed the vase of flowers she had picked on her walk on the sideboard beneath them. For a short while the lamplight threw about wild waving shadows.

"Mom used to say that wallspiders bring rain." Susanna pushed past the large sofa to straighten the stern portrait. Johannes stood at the door ready to flee.

"Come on Dad, sit down," Susanna patted the chair and he shuffled towards the sofa and felt his body relax as he sank into the soft dusty velvet.

"This reminds me of when you used to hide in your study and Mom and I used to light all the lamps. She'd tell me wonderful stories." Pushing open the heavy curtains, she lifted the fly screen and opened the windows. "This place smells like a museum and besides it's hot." She wiped her forehead and lit a cigarette.

Johannes looked at his hands and closed his eyes. This eternal sadness. Where did it come from?

"I miss her so much tonight." Susanna pulled heavily on her cigarette. "I wish I'd brought some wine."

The lamp light was always soothing.

"Where's that photograph of you and Auntie Anna at the studio in Louis Trichardt?"

Johannes shrugged his shoulders.

"I think you should replace the old folks with that one." She looked at the portrait of Mutti and Father again, grimacing.

"You didn't understand him."

"I saw how he treated Mom." The reply came back sharply.

"Yes," Johannes said. "After four years in the camp Father never did trust the English."

She was looking for something, opening all the doors of the big cupboard. He wished she would settle down. Finally she found what she was looking for.

"Sweet Jerepigo! It'll have to do."

"It was your Grandfather's. It's communion wine." Johannes smiled faintly. "Think it came with the furniture."

Susanna giggled and wiped the dust off the bottle with her dress. She poured the dark red liquid right to the brim. Before he could protest, she had passed him a glass. Johannes took it carefully, managing to spill some on his fresh shirt.

"Sorry." There was a slight hysteria in her laugh. "I made it too full!"

He tried to wipe off the stain with his free hand but only spilled more.

"Here's to Wilhelm Weber.' Susanna raised her glass. "The Infallible!"

Johannes didn't feel like protesting. He drank some and could feel the heady sweetness radiate throughout his body.

"Sometimes you were such a strange child," he said, unable to stop the smile. "Always closing your ears and humming when I spoke about him."

"That's because you were trying to convince me how wonderful Grandfather was," she said, raising her glass towards the darkening portrait. "Meanwhile he was actually an arsehole. Never accepted Mom. Never could see what the missionaries were actually doing."

Johannes put down his glass. He would have to go and fetch a wet cloth to wipe the Jerepigo off his shirt.

"Relax, Dad. Let's get drunk tonight." Susana jumped up and started rummaging in the drawers of the sideboard again. "Found it!" She held up the small leather cushion that fitted neatly into her hand. "The rhythm cushion!" She lifted it to her nose. "I always loved this smell."

She started to beat it, singing at the top of her voice. She danced around the table once, then stopped.

"Shit, there's hardly any space to move around inside here with this bloody old Berlin furniture." The lamps flickered as she sat down on the sofa next to him.

"Jesus, remember when they delivered it? I can still hear Mom saying: 'It'll squeeze us all out of this house, Johannes.'

Remember?" Susanna closed her eyes.

"I never come in here much." Johannes looked around him. They were silent for a while. She looked so different in this light, her hair loose and soft, her eyes sparkling.

"Do you remember our trip to Wittenberg?" His voice was already slurring.

"Of course."

"You were only four."

"I'd never seen so many butterflies before." Her face was glowing. "Mom told me they were Auntie Anna's fairies. We were sitting under this huge tree, I think it was in the graveyard, watching them drift by while you were pacing about complaining how everything had changed - ruined, was the word you used - since Grandfather left."

"He always said that one couldn't hand anything over to the blacks."

"What did he expect, Dad? The Berlin Mission Society withdrew all the funding overnight." Susanna got up to fetch the bottle of Jerepigo from the sideboard and filled their glasses again. "How were the congregations supposed to look after the buildings without money?"

"Still - they could have tried." Father was looking even more sternly at him now. Probably was cross that they were drinking the communion wine.

Susanna took her glass to the window and lit another cigarette. "You should have seen the old Lutheran mission station in Tanzania. It was beautiful with huge trees all around. Quite uncanny, it was almost the same design as Wittenberg. Even the church looked the same, just painted yellow and blue. Same square tower."

"They had a standard design for mission churches in those days." He should go and look for the photograph of Anna. That trip to the studio in Louis Trichardt, he could remember it vividly. Mutti had wanted to send Father a picture of the family for Christmas. Willie was sick so he had to stay at home. Mutti had plaited Anna's hair into two pretty monkey swings. Of course Anna asked why Noria and Thambulo couldn't come as well, and as usual Mutti was exasperated with her. They had spent hours in the studio. He most liked the photograph with only Anna and him in it. It showed how hard he had tried to smile for Father but the jacket and long pants had made him feel so uncomfortable. Anna, on the other, hand, looked straight at the camera with that slightly mistrustful and defiant look. The picture captured her well.

"It was funny, you know, Tanzania brought back so many memories." Susanna tried to wave away the smoke of her cigarette, but it only coiled back into the room. "When I got back to the conference after I'd been to the mission station I didn't feel like speaking to anyone. And then those delegates started with their shit."

"The Vhavenda have a saying, that sooner or later nature will get rid of any intruders," Johannes said. "They meant the Europeans."

"I got so angry. Told them the culling programmes they were proposing weren't so different to the Holocaust." She combed her hair with her hand. She used to do that sometimes when she was a child. "So, one of my colleagues comes to me during the break and says I mustn't be so aggressive and that I alienate people. I told him they could fuck themselves if they didn't want to hear the truth."

She lit another cigarette and took a gulp of Jerepigo. "The worst was, I made such a mess of my paper. Jesus, I just couldn't hold the audience. And I'm usually good at that." She put out the cigarette and emptied her glass. "After question time I just went to the toilet and cried."

"Me too," Johannes said. "Father always said that Willie carried his bladder between his ears, but nowadays it's me. All the time the tears just want to come."

"Ja, Dad." Susanna sat down next to him on the sofa, pouring the last bit of Jerepigo into their glasses. She put her arm on the headrest behind him. "I think I can understand you hiding in the study a bit better now. I feel happiest when I'm alone with my computer." She pushed one of the lamps aside and put her feet up onto the coffee table. "Jesus, Dad, sometimes you were in there the whole night. What were you doing?"

"Couldn't sleep. Still can't." He pointed outside towards the car wreck. "Nowadays it's that woman who keeps me awake."

"I take sleeping pills most nights," Susanna confessed. "I can give you some."

"She makes me think of Venda." A breeze caused the flames to flicker dangerously. "Sometimes I think she wants me gone so that she can move in here." He tried to pull himself out of the sofa, but he couldn't and fell back again. "Grace says she's a rainmaker, but I don't know."

"Like the Holumbe?"

"No, like the Malombo women." He could feel his water rising again and sighed. He finally managed to get up. "The Holumbe didn't make rain."

When he got back to the lounge Susanna was holding the rhythm cushion again.

"I wish we had some music." She started to beat it. "You used to sing so beautifully, Dad." She started marching noisily among the furniture. *"Daughter of Ziooon, Rejoice."*

"Who the hell is the daughter of Zion?" She stopped in front of him.

"I don't know."

"Remember when you said you would throw away the rhythm cushion and I said I would never talk to you again if you did that?"

Johannes sank back into the sofa and smiled wearily. "You always did get your way, though. Like Anna."

"Come dance with me, Dad." Susana tried to pull him up, but he couldn't get up so fast. She let go of him and fell against the table. A lamp shattered and a flame escaped, quickly licking up the stream of paraffin, making its way to the velvet curtains.

"Shit!" Susanna jumped aside. The flames seized the curtains, like a monkey ready to swing from object to object. Johannes sat rooted to the sofa. All he could do was watch her - dancing wildly with the monkey, leaping across the coffee table and pulling sharply at the curtains which came crashing down onto the floor. She stomped and trampled but the monkey refused to die. She grabbed a velvet cushion from the armchair and beat at the flames, which flared up from her effort. Soot and stuffing were flying everywhere.

Finally she tamed it. Suffocated it.

"Jesus!" She started to laugh, wiping her eyes. "I've always been so bloody clumsy."

"You put that fire out fast." Johannes said admiringly. Father and Mother Weber continued to stare across the room. He wanted to laugh and dance and sing.

"We nearly burnt it all down!" He wanted to shout, but the smoke filled his eyes with tears. Then he noticed blood on Susanna's ankle. "Maybe we should put on the lights," he said, pointing at her leg.

Susanna shook her head and bent down to wipe away the blood with her hand. "Just a little cut," she coughed and started to pick up the pieces of glass from the floor.

"I've always hated those curtains." He could feel the laughter rising in his belly again. "Missionary Els brought them for Mutti during the war. He was always a bit too nice to her for my liking. He probably hoped that Father wouldn't come back from Andalusia – funny, I've never thought of that before."

Susanna went to fetch a brush and dustpan. When she came back into lounge there was a dangerous glint in her eyes. "If you want to, we can burn more things. Just keep the rhythm cushion."

"Yes!" said Johannes. "Let's make a big fire!" Susanna went to the sideboard to look for more wine, but there wasn't any. Instead she found the old record player.

"How does this work again, Dad?"

He wanted to get up and show her but everything was spinning and the room smelt heavily of smoke and paraffin. Then the soft, close harmonies of the African Gospel Singers enveloped the room and Susanna began moving her body to the music. Johannes closed his eyes and rested his head against the sofa. This music always made him want to cry. His hand found the rhythm cushion lying next to him, he picked it up and felt the familiar leathery smoothness in his hands. Putting his hand through the loop, he slowly started to beat it. Somehow he lifted himself out of the sofa and began to shuffle about the room. And then the words rose in his throat.

"Abide with us," he sang along, *"for it is eventide."*

"Shit," he heard Susanna say. "I've probably burnt the pasta."

We visit **Father**

School isn't too bad. Mutti says that Anna and I are very clever and that we learn fast. Reading, writing, counting, adding and general knowledge – we can do them all already. She says that from July she will ask Miss Talbot to teach us a bit of English and Afrikaans.

Miss Talbot is Mutti's new friend. She is from Scotland and is helping her brother who runs the Salvation Army clinic near Sibasa. Mutti says that if we learn English and Afrikaans fast enough, then from next year we can follow the Education Department syllabus.

One day after the July holidays, the car that the Mission Society promised us arrives. It is a second-hand green Ford. Mutti says we are very lucky to get one and that now we don't have to depend on Missionary Els so much. He is teaching her to drive and it isn't too difficult, she tells me. Mutti says I am too small to drive.

Once she practises driving down the road and then, when we're already past Maharaj's, she doesn't know how to turn the car around again, so Anna and I have to get out and run to the shop to go and fetch Mr Maharaj to help us.

But now Mutti can drive much better. Sometimes she drives to Sibasa to visit Miss Talbot or she fetches her so that she can visit and teach us English. But Miss Talbot doesn't really teach us much because Mutti and her spend the whole day talking, even though Mutti can't speak English that well either and Miss Talbot wants to learn some German.

Mutti says that she's going to save up petrol coupons for November because we've got permission to go and visit Father in Andalusia on the 30th of November. It's really nice because we can see him again the next day for the Christmas visit because it will be the 1st of December. Besides, we have to do it soon, Mutti says, because only children under seven are allowed to visit and I'm already seven and almost eight.

Mutti closes our school two weeks early for the holidays so we can get to Andalusia on time. The journey to Kimberley is very long. First we drive to Pietersburg with our car and leave it at the Bishop's house, then the bishop takes us to the station so that we can catch the train to Pretoria. At night we get onto the train to Kimberley.

In Pretoria we're joined on the train by an auntie who is going to visit her husband in the camp. He is not a missionary but a butcher.

The auntie tells us that she's going to try to get her husband out of Andalusia because he has asthma. Mutti says she wishes Father wasn't so very healthy so she could do the same. The auntie says she doesn't wish asthma on her worst enemy.

While the auntie puts on her nightdress we have to stand in the passage. Mutti tells us that the woman couldn't have children because something is wrong with her eggs. She also tells us not to speak German too loud in the train because of the war and that some people don't like Germans. Anna and I decide to speak Tshivenda instead and a man with a big moustache squeezes past us and looks at us funny. Mutti then says maybe we shouldn't speak Tshivenda either.

The auntie is fat so she has to sleep on the bottom bunk. Anna and I are allowed to sleep on the top bunk and Mutti sleeps in the other bottom bunk with Willie. In the night the auntie snores very loud, like a man. And Anna and I start to giggle. Mutti gets up and tells us to keep quiet.

Early in the morning the auntie wakes up and opens the shutters. Everything is flat with only a few bushes. The sun makes everything look golden. A man knocks on our door, selling hot coffee and tea. It's very nice coffee and Mutti says it is because it has condensed milk in it.

When we get closer to Kimberley Anna wants to know where the diamonds are. Mutti laughs and the auntie says that Anna is a very impatient little girl. Then she gets up to fetch her bag from the top and farts loud. Mutti looks at us sternly to make sure that we don't laugh. The auntie opens the window. It's cold outside. Mutti says it's because Kimberley is like a desert – cold at night and hot in the day.

As soon as we get to the station Anna wants to go and see Father. Mutti rolls her eyes at the auntie and reminds Anna that we are first going to visit Pastor Schroeder and then three more sleeps and then he will take us to Andalusia.

Pastor Schroeder is waiting for us at the station in a car that is much bigger than ours. He says he needs it because he has six children. It's nice at their house because Tante Schroeder isn't strict like Muttie and we're allowed to stay up as late as we like and play. The Schroeder children have lots of toys that they let us play with.

The next day Pastor Schroeder takes us all to the Big Hole in Kimberley where they are still digging for diamonds. It's a very big hole and far down in the middle of it there is water. You can't see the diamonds though. To see diamonds you have to go to the museum where they also have lots of old pictures of all the people collecting soil to get diamonds.

In church on Sunday there are many Germans and Pastor Schroeder prays for all the men in the camp and for their families. Outside the church everyone greets us. There are other people too who have come to see their fathers in Andalusia. One woman asks if I'm not a bit too big to be visiting my father.

"He's just very tall," Mutti lies. "Like me."

On Monday Pastor Schroeder drives us to Andalusia. Mutti is very nervous. She's left Willie with Tante Schroeder and she keeps telling me that I must try to look young but I don't know how to do that.

Mutti says it's better if we already think about what we are going to say to Father when we see him. I want to tell him about Thambulo. Anna and I have also prepared a poem for Father but Pastor Schroeder tells us that the last time he brought someone to Andalusia the visitors had to stand far away from the internees.

By the time we finally get to the camp it's very hot. Andalusia is a big place with two high fences right around it and on top of the fences are rolls of barbed wire. There are towers all along the fence with soldiers with real guns sitting in them. The buildings inside all look the same except for a few in the front. Pastor Schroeder explains that those are the offices and dining rooms and that the rest are the barracks where the men sleep. We park the car next to some other cars and then walk to the guardhouse at the big gates where other people are already waiting. Pastor Schroeder goes to speak English to an unfriendly soldier.

"I'm scared," I tell Mutti.

"Try to look young," she whispers.

Another soldier comes. He looks at me sternly but tells Mutti to write down our names and address in a book. I can see that her hands are shaking. Then he tells us to go to another place to wait.

When we get to the place where we are going to see Father, there are many other people waiting as well. It's very hot and there are no trees. Mutti says she should have brought some hats and a flask with cold water.

"Are we going to see Father just now?" asks Anna.

Mutti holds onto Anna's shoulders tightly and Anna keeps trying to wriggle free. Pastor Schroeder says we could wait in the shade of the car, but Mutti says she's not willing to take that chance.

"You're so quiet, Hannes," Mutti rubs my hair. "Are you looking forward to seeing your father?"

I nod. More people arrive. There are soldiers marching between the fences. Anna wants to know where Father is going to be. One woman looks at me and tells Mutti that I'm very tall for a six year old. Mutti is annoyed and pulls me closer. I bend my knees a bit so that I look shorter.

Another woman is holding a little boy on her arm. He is crying so much that his face has turned bright red. She explains that he is teething but she decided to still bring him because the father has never seen his own son before. Then everybody is quiet because some soldiers with guns stop right in front of us and face us.

"They're coming," whispers Pastor Schroeder. We move closer to the fence.

Finally a line of men in khaki shorts and shirts emerges from the big barrack.

"There he is," shouts Mutti. Pastor Schroeder lifts Anna onto his shoulders.

The men line up behind the soldiers. I can't see Father.

"There! Wave!" Mutti is excited and Anna and I wave frantically. There are many men waving.

Some of the women are shouting for the soldiers to move out of the way so they can see their husbands.

"How are you?" Mutti shouts at someone. But he looks a lot smaller than Father.

"Hannes and Anna practised a poem for you," Mutti says. "But I don't know how they are going to say it for you."

The man lifts his hands to his ears to show that he can't hear what Mutti is saying.

"Wave Hannes," she says. Pastor Schroeder puts down Anna and lifts me up.

"The children are very good," Mutti shouts.

The man says something back. His skin is red and his hair is very short. He looks at me and smiles and says something. Pastor Schroeder says I'm a bit too heavy and puts me down again.

"Tomorrow I'm going to bring little Willie," Mutti says, wiping her eyes.

I want to see the man smile at me again but all I can see are the soldiers and I feel a bit sick. After a while a man blows a whistle and the soldiers tell the men to line up and stop talking. Pastor Schroeder lifts Anna up again and I can see Father blowing us a kiss.

"That wasn't half an hour," a woman shouts at the soldiers.

The others agree and we all move towards the big guardhouse at the gate and the loud woman demands to see the camp commander.

"He isn't here," the soldier says.

"That's a lie!" she shouts at him.

He tells us all to go now but no one is moving. I'm holding Anna's hand.

"This is not what we were promised," the woman shouts. "Tomorrow I'm going to bring a Red Cross representative and then you'll all be in trouble."

Slowly we move back to the cars. Pastor Schroeder has his arm around Mutti. The car is very hot.

"Wave!" Mutti says as we drive off. So we wave again and Anna starts to cry.

"At least he looks healthy," Mutti says in a brave voice.

Pastor Schroeder says that when we get to Kimberley he is going to take us to a tearoom so that we can eat ice cream. But still Anna can't stop crying.

"Why are there no trees in Andalusia?" I ask.

"He looks so handsome," Mutti says.

The next day Mutti goes to visit Father with Willie. She says it will be easier if we don't come along and neither Anna nor I argue with her.

We spend the whole day playing with the toys. When Mutti comes back she says it was much better this time because there were fewer soldiers and she and Father had a full half hour to talk. She says that Father is keeping body and soul together by studying and by participating in lots of sports. He's doing gymnastics and football.

"I said your poem for him and he liked it a lot."

At night Mutti goes to bed early because she has a headache. We walk with the family Schroeder to a big red school where they are showing moving pictures. It's like a story book but with real people. Before they start, a lady plays 'God save the King' on the piano and we all have to stand up.

The next day we have to say goodbye. Mutti is very quiet all the way back from Kimberley to Pretoria and from Pretoria to Pietersburg. Anna and I play with Willie so that he doesn't bother her too much.

When we finally get home Anna and I are very happy to see Thambulo and Noria and Asta, and Mukegulu Wilhelmina and VhoSarah as well. We tell them about Kimberley and the big hole with the diamonds in it. I give Thambulo a stone that I picked up in Kimberley. Pastor Schroeder said it's a semi-precious stone, almost like a diamond.

Mutti goes and lies in her room for a few days and only when Miss Talbot comes to visit does she manage to get herself out of bed again.

10.

Another bad night. She'd have to go to town and organise a fresh supply of sleeping pills from the local GP. She never slept that well in this house but she'd hoped that the Jerepigo would help.

Susanna pulled aside the dusty curtains and looked outside at the cloudless morning. There was probably no chance of rain today. There had been no woman praying and singing at the car wreck in the night either – she hadn't heard a thing between bouts of bad dreams and lying awake and thinking. It was probably another of Dad's paranoid ideas - like the snakes hiding under the house.

The house smelt of smoke and paraffin, but at least they'd had a good evening together last night. He was getting softer with age, opening up a bit.

The kitchen looked terrible. It would take hours to get it properly cleaned, wash the walls, scrub the floor, clean the stove, re-wash all the dishes, throw stuff out. She should ask someone to help her with the cleaning. It was hard enough to get Dad to throw anything away. What he needed was someone to come and clean at least once a week, but he'd probably refuse. He never wanted to let anyone clean the house at Witrivier either, said it had something to do with growing up in Venda. She didn't understand him much.

Susanna lit a cigarette and stared at the kettle for a while, looking at her distorted reflection. Now she remembered what she had dreamt about - Prince. They had gone for a walk together, like in the old days. No wonder she was feeling so sad this morning.

Taking the big bunch of keys out of the breadbin, she unlocked the front door, but when it came to the security gate it refused to budge. She tried again and again, but it was no use. She would have to take her coffee into the lounge and drink it there.

The place was a mess with pillow stuffing and ash everywhere. The curtains looked tattered like old bats. It was a miracle they hadn't burnt the place down completely. She smiled and flopped down onto the big sofa. The windows were filthy, they probably hadn't been washed since Dad moved in here seven years ago. At least now she could see outside.

Grandfather and Grandmother were irritating her more than usual in their frame this morning so she got up and took down the portrait. Where was that picture of Auntie Anna and Dad? It was a brilliant photograph, capturing something in them – Auntie Anna looking defiantly at the camera and Dad shy and uncertain - like children who seldom came to town. Mom had insisted on hanging the photo in their lounge in Witrivier, but Dad had probably hidden it now. He was so weird about Auntie Anna, and never wanting to visit her, even though Mom said she thought they had been incredibly close.

Susanna lit another cigarette. Maybe she should start cleaning up this room. She could always do the kitchen later when Dad was awake. She had to try and include him, otherwise he would get angry like last time.

Susanna went to fetch a broom and black rubbish bags and slowly she began to gather the debris, taking down the remnants of the singed curtains. Her dream wouldn't leave her, the feeling of it. She had gone walking up into the koppies when suddenly Prince had come bounding up to her. She was so pleased to see him again, even though she knew he had died long ago. He was running through the veld, sniffing the grass and rocks, and then, when they had got to the top, he had vanished towards the grove of sweet-thorns, probably looking for the buck. She had called him and called, but he didn't come back. She had stood there, at the top of the koppie, and her heart had ached so much that she had woken up from the pain.

As she continued sweeping the floor Susanna could feel the old resentments rising in her. Dad had been such an arsehole. He hadn't even had the guts to wait for Mom and her to get back from taking Maureen to the station before shooting Prince. He said that it was too dangerous. Prince was acting strange, barking at him and foaming at the mouth, he had said.

"It's because *you* are weird that he barked at you, Dad. There was nothing wrong with Prince. It was you who spooked him," she'd screamed at him. "It's you who acted strange."

"He was foaming at the mouth and last week Franz Muller shot a rabid rabbit," he had replied. "One can't take a chance."

She was sobbing violently, Mom held her close. "Tell him, Mom, tell him that he should have waited for me."

"I couldn't take a chance," he had repeated. "He could have bitten you too."

"He wouldn't have," she protested.

But Dad had already buried Prince under the avocado tree, one of Prince's favourite places to lie on a hot day. She had demanded to see the grave and Dad followed her. After looking at the mound of earth for a while, Susanna turned around and faced him.

"It could have been jackal poison, Dad, that made him foam at the mouth. Did you ever think about that?" she spat out. "Jackal poison that *you* put out!" And then she ran into her room and stayed there till Mom fetched her for supper.

A week later Susanna had gone into his office one afternoon and tore up the forestry journals he had ordered from Germany and had studied night after night. Then she tore up the pages and pages of records of rain and plantings he had so meticulously kept and triumphantly scattered the pieces all over his room. For almost a year afterwards she never spoke to him, and her resolve never broke. Even when he offered to buy her a horse, she simply ignored him. God knows, she had wanted to punish him.

Susanna took the black bags into the passage. She needed to get some fresh air, to take the bags outside and pull herself together. All this shit was coming back to her, like residual poison, spoiling the fun they had had last night. She tried again to unlock the security door, but it was no use. She started to rattle at it, she didn't care. He had to wake up now and let her out of here.

Bismarck and the Mamba

Father had a horse called Bismarck, but I can't remember him because I was too small. It was before the war. Father said Bismarck was a magnificent horse, big and as black as the night. When Bismarck was angry he used to shake his mane and flare his nostrils. Everybody was afraid of him, but not Father.

Father used to take Bismarck everywhere to inspect the mission farms around Wittenberg and to visit the far away outstations. At first Bismarck was stubborn and he used to try to get Father off his back by running under low branches. But Father is a farmer's son and is very strong! Father had tamed many horses in Germany before he came to Venda, so when Bismarck tried to buck him off, he just held onto the reigns and dug in his heels. Sometimes there was even blood on the spurs and Bismarck flashed his eyes and frothed at the mouth and shook and reared up, but Father stayed on his back and rode him for hours and hours every day.

My favourite story about Bismarck is the one when Father went to visit a chief up north because the chief had sent a message that he wanted to be christened.

"Never before, during my time in Africa had this happened," Father told me. "Even though I knew that it was probably his favourite wife who was behind the request, I didn't mind. When a chief wants to be christened, you have to oblige him, because it means that many more souls will be won for Jesus Christ."

Father prepared for the long and hard journey all the way around the Soutpansberge and up north where it is hot and dry. He travelled with his Zulu evangelist, David, who drove the mule and cart while Father rode on Bismarck. At first they travelled through the forests and jungles with monkey-vines as thick as your arms. Then they got to the hot dry bush where there were baobab trees. In those days you could not travel without a gun. There were still many wild animals roaming around and you had to keep your eyes open for lions, leopards, wild pigs, buck and even elephants, although there weren't that many of those left. Djambo was one of the last elephants around Wittenberg.

Father told me that on that trip it had rained a lot, even in the dry country. This caused Father and Evangelist David to be on the road for three days longer than they had expected, struggling through the mud and the swelling rivers. It was already Sunday morning, the day of the christening, when they finally reached the Moane River that flows into the great Limpopo. The chief's homestead was just on the other side of the river. As they stood there, right in front of their eyes the river started to rise, thick and brown and angry. Without hesitating, Father took the little case with the Holy Communion utensils out of the wagon and rode into the Moane with Bismarck. He held the case high in the air above his head as Bismarck swam across the raging torrent. Evangelist David, his mouth wide open, watched the two from the banks of the river.

"Join us as soon as you can," Father shouted back to him.

On the other side of the river he was met by the astonished tribesmen. When he rode with Bismarck into the chief's kraal, the people knelt before him, but Father told them that the only one they should bend their knees to was God.

Later Father found out that their most powerful witchdoctor had predicted that the ancestors would not allow this man to come and baptise their chief. "Nature will kill these white ants that are invading our land," he had said.

"They really believed that the ancestors had sent a flood to stop God's work," Father had laughed.

And so, although Father's black Luther robe was wet and muddy from the crossing, the chief's baptism could begin on time. Father liked things to be punctual.

From then on, Father never went anywhere without Bismarck and the horse became famous all over Venda. Father said that his horse was the best evangelist he ever had. The people thought that a missionary who could tame a horse like that must have had strong medicine!

Bismarck even had a lion's paw marks on his right shank. That happened when Evangelist David and Father were camping out in the forest. They had tied up the horse and the mule a bit further away, and then, in the middle of the night while they were sleeping, a pride of lions came and brought down the mule. Bismarck fought them off but unfortunately they carried off the mule. Father said that Evangelist David had to stop him from pursuing those lions on Bismarck.

Sometimes in the olden days before he was married, Father would go right into Mashonaland, like the old missionaries used to. On these trips he would be away from Wittenberg for weeks on end. At night he and his evangelists would camp out in the veld near a village. Father would shoot an animal and roast it on the fire and invite the people to come and eat. Many came because they had not often seen a white man. After the meal, when everybody was relaxed, Father would tell them stories from the Bible.

Mutti says that Father knows how to move people and that he speaks better Tshivenda than the Vhavenda themselves. Before he went to Andalusia he used to spend hours in his study at night, translating hymns from German into Tshivenda.

"You must just imagine this, Hannes," Father used to tell this story with his whole body.

"Around the fire are sitting the higher-ranking men. The lesser ranking men sit behind them. Further outside sit the women. And right outside the circle are the young girls." Father's eyes shone. "When these girls heard the Holy Gospel they really felt it in their hearts." Father beat his chest to show how the Gospel can enter through the heart. "It is because in their society they count as nothing!" Father flicked his hand in mock dismissal. "And then sometimes after listening to the word of God, it stirred them and they would beg their parents to let them become Christians."

Sarah came to us from one of those trips. Her family had already received gifts from the husband-to-be, who was an ugly old man with many wives and she did not want to marry him.

"I asked the Mufunzi to take me with him. 'Please Vhafunzi,' I pleaded. 'I will die if you don't take me with you. I am going to walk into Lake Fundudzi and let the spirits take me." VhoSarah laughs a lot when she tells this story. "I was such a silly girl!" She wipes her eyes with the back of her hands. "But luckily the Mufunzi was looking for good Christian wives for his teachers and evangelists."

"Then why haven't you married?" Anna asks.

"Because I am working here in your house now," Sarah laughs and taps Anna on the nose. "And I don't need a husband and a family because I have got you!"

She tells us how Father gave her family money so that she could come and stay with us. Anna and I move closer to Sarah, we are happy that Father saved her from marrying that smelly old man.

"Tell us about when your husband-to-be came here to Wittenberg to try to take you back home." Anna likes hearing that part of the story.

Sarah claps her hands. "He came in the middle of the night to my hut and tried to force me to go with him. 'You are mine,' he said. 'No,' I told him. 'I don't belong to anyone.'"

"Tell me again, what did he look like?" Anna's eyes grow bigger.

"He was so ugly. Some of his front teeth were missing and the rest were yellow and crooked and his beard was thin and dirty. You should have seen his hands." Anna is disgusted. "They were too big for his small body. And he smelt like an old Kaross!"

Anna and Sarah laugh until the tears run down their faces. They always laugh. Sarah is beautiful. I wish I could marry her but Mutti says it's not possible.

One day a terrible thing happened to Bismarck. Father had gone to visit Chief Tshivase to discuss building a church near his kraal. He had also wanted to persuade him to keep only one wife because the chief was setting a bad example to the Christians.

Father told us that it was a difficult visit because the chief had just laughed at Father and told him to mind his own business. He would allow the Mufunzi to talk about his God, but he couldn't tell him anything about his customs. But at least he had agreed to build a church on the hill overlooking the main homestead. On the way back from the visit, Father rode Bismarck hard.

"I wanted to be home with Mutti. It was the rainy season and she was sick all during the time that Anna was in her tummy."

"Was Mutti also sick when I was in her tummy?" I asked.

"No," said Father. "I don't think so."

I wanted to ask more questions but Father continued: "I remember it so clearly. I was only a few hours away from Wittenberg. Bismarck and I had been riding for five hours already so I decided to take a break at the river. While I was waiting for the kettle to boil on the fire I lay down under a feverberry tree. I could hear Bismarck grazing behind me and then I must have dozed off."

Father got up and paced the room when he told us the story. "Suddenly I wake up. Bismarck was whinnying out loudly. I turned towards him and then I saw it - out of a large termite mound came a huge black mamba, the biggest one I had ever seen - almost ten feet long!" Father pointed to the top of a nearby pine to show us how tall the snake was.

"It sailed straight at me, its front reared up high." Father turned his hand into a gaping snake mouth. "I'll never forget its black coffin-shaped mouth, and the sound of the hissing. And that flickering black tongue."

Anna and I shuddered.

"It was coming straight towards me and there was no time to take aim and shoot." He paused.

"Next, I saw Bismarck rearing up, chopping at that messenger of Satan. It was a magnificent fight between the snake and the horse. I had never seen such a thing before. I swear there were sparks flying out of that stallion's hooves, and the snake repeatedly lunged at him, hissing. Finally Bismarck struck it such a blow that the snake lay crushed in the mud." Father wiped his brow, his arms sank to his sides.

"It was all over in a few minutes, but when I got close to Bismarck, I saw the fang marks on his knees and neck." Now Father wiped his eyes as he spoke. "The poison took effect quickly."

I shut my ears with my hands for a bit because I knew what was going to happen next.

"And then he looked into my eyes," Father continued. "Bismarck was pleading with me." He wiped away a tear. "And I had to do it. I had to shoot my best friend and most loyal companion."

Mutti had joined us on the veranda. "Are you telling the children that terrible story again, Wilhelm?" she admonished him and hooked her arm through his.

"I want our children to understand true valour, Elisabeth."

Mutti looked at him, smiling. "Your poor Father! When he came home there wasn't even time to tell me what had happened because I had gone into labour with Anna. He had to rush me to the hospital in Louis Trichardt immediately." Mutti pulled Anna closely towards her. "And then the next day, on the 19th of October 1936, my little girl was born."

Anna squirmed and tried to get out of Mutti's grip.

11

There's a monkey in a cage at the entrance of the photographer's studio. Anna wants to go and touch it but Mutti says it'll bite her.

"But it's sad," says Anna.

"Never mind," says Mutti. "We have to take your picture now. Father is waiting."

The monkey rattles the door of the cage. Anna holds out her hand towards it. The monkey shows its teeth. "It's dangerous, Anna," Johannes warns her.

Anna keeps her hand stretched out. The monkey takes it and starts to grin. It's very happy.

"Come, Anna," Mutti calls from inside. "We can't keep Father waiting any longer."

Johannes wonders if Father is inside the studio. Anna lets go of the monkey's hand. It gets very upset and starts to rattle the cage again.

"See what you've done," he wants to say to her.

And then he woke up.

The sun was shining through the thin curtains straight onto his bed. Must be late already. He looked at the alarm clock. Ten past eight! Goodness. Hadn't slept this late in a long time. Must have been the Jerepigo. Johannes smiled and closed his eyes again. She could be quite wild, his Susanna.

The rattling started again. It was coming from the passage.

"These fucking keys! I can't get the door open."

Johannes pushed aside the blanket and lifted himself up. He carefully got out of bed, his head thick and throbbing. There was something strange about the light this morning, all yellow, like after a fire. Yes, he remembers, there had been a fire. Slowly he picked up his clothes from the floor. He'd wear them again today. Saves washing them, wearing them out. Slowly, walking towards the mirror of the big wooden wardrobe he pulled a comb through his thin hair. He smiled at the big red Jerepigo stain across his shirt.

The rattling continued. He should probably go and rescue her, poor girl always so impatient.

"Just a minute," he shouted as he put on a fresh shirt. His body was stiff and achy.

The passage smelled of paraffin.

"Jesus, I've been struggling with these keys for hours already, Dad, I need to get out!" Susanna looked tired and pale. She was wearing a pair of faded jeans and a large khaki shirt, working clothes. Her unruly hair was tied up with a piece of red cloth she must have found in one of the cupboards.

"Just have to go to the toilet."

As soon as he came out of the bathroom she followed him into the passage and watched as he struggled with the keys. She was standing close behind him, her irritation rising.

"We've got to sort through your keys today, Dad. It's like you've kept every single key you've ever owned."

Finally the security door opened and Susanna picked up the black bags she had piled near the door and went outside. He knew better not to ask her what she was throwing away. Much better idea to get himself a cup of coffee.

Johannes found Susanna on the veranda smoking, glancing impatiently at her cell phone.

"Nobody ever answers their phone before ten on Fridays. We could get so much more done in this country if everybody stopped spending their workdays in meetings."

He wished she would settle down a bit. Let him get used to the bright morning light. Drink his coffee in peace. It tasted good. He couldn't remember when last he'd slept so well. Father must be turning in his grave, getting drunk on communion wine like that!

"How did you sleep?" Johannes asked cautiously.

"Terribly! I woke up in the middle of the night and thought of all the things I need to do."

It was going to be another hot day. Better to stay inside.

Susanna's phone rang. She answered it immediately and started walking towards the kitchen. Even though she closed the doors behind her, her voice carried through the house. She was obviously arguing with someone.

"You can forget it!" She was banging the kitchen cupboards,

moving things about. "I won't apologise to those people." It was quiet for a while and the phone rang again and the arguing continued.

When he went back inside he felt like going to look for the photograph of him and Anna. What an odd dream. Couldn't remember when last he had dreamt. Kate had said he just never remembered his dreams.

The lounge looked strange without the curtains, naked. Susanna had obviously been in here tidying up. Johannes sat down on the sofa. The dust danced about him in the yellow light. He watched it settle. Everything looked so faded. There was a white blotch on the wall - where did Father and Mutti's photograph go? Maybe Susanna was right, it was time to get rid of the old Berlin furniture. You could hardly move in here.

She had stopped talking on the phone and walked out the front door again. He wished she would calm down a bit. He couldn't talk to her about Father's kist when she was in this mood. All that history, it would be a pity if everything got thrown away.

He could see her now, standing outside on the lawn near the fence, talking to someone. He fetched the binoculars from the sideboard. It was Grace; she must have been passing by. Susanna looked like a man in those jeans. She was gesticulating and pointing at the house, talking and smiling as if she had been in a good mood all morning. She looked so much like Father when he was supervising the building or the farm. Grace seemed to be writing something down, while Pulane stood by, looking bored. No sign of the woman. Maybe it was she who had kept Susanna awake – singing and praying.

Johannes sat down on the sofa again. He was so tired. He would just sink into the sofa for a bit. Close his eyes and go back to Anna. It was probably Advent soon. Maybe they could make a wreath and light the candles. Sing around the piano. Maybe he should go and get himself another cup of coffee before Susanna came back inside again. But it was too late already. He heard her on the veranda.

"Dad?" There was an urgency in her voice. "Dad!"

Just a few moments of quiet.

Now she was moving things around in the kitchen and Johannes wondered whether he had ever told her about Bismarck. She'd loved horses as a child.

"Dad, where are you?" She called again. "Come and help me sort through the kitchen cupboards."

He would slip outside quietly. Go and feed the birds. Sit in the garage for a bit. Rest. It was nice and dark in there.

"What are you doing in here, Dad?"

She was wearing yellow rubber gloves now, carrying a box filled with paint tins and brushes and tools, a thick strand of greying hair creeping out from under her scarf. "I've been looking for you everywhere."

"Feeding the birds." He must have fallen asleep on the sack of seeds. The little red cup was resting in his lap.

"I've just come to bring all the hardware stuff from the kitchen in here." Her voice had softened a little since this morning. "God, it's dark in here." She flicked on the light switch. The neon light hurt his eyes.

"Are you sure you're all right, Dad? You look a bit pale."

Johannes shrugged his shoulders.

"I met that woman Grace earlier." She put down the box she was carrying. "She's wonderful. You never told me about her. Do you know she used to be a nurse?"

He had to feed the birds. They had probably given up already and flown away.

"She says she keeps offering to help you but you refuse."

"I don't need anyone." He wished Susanna would leave things alone.

"Dad, your house is a mess!" She stood in front of the shelves full of gardening things and started picking up bottles and boxes and packets, reading their labels. "Anyhow, I've arranged for her to come next week to help me. I'll pay for it."

Johannes braced himself. "Your mother and I have never had anyone cleaning our house and I don't want anyone now either."

She ignored him, scanning the shelves. "I can't believe the amount of poisons you keep in here."

He was going to get angry soon.

She took down an empty apple box and started throwing things from the shelf into it.

"Those are my things from Witrivier. I want you to leave them alone."

"Most of this stuff has expired, Dad, and some of it's been banned ages ago." Susanna held up a small see-through bottle with a faded red label. "Jesus, did you know that this causes breast cancer in birds? I'm going to have to take these to Joburg with me and have them disposed of. These things are dangerous." She shook her head in disgust. "What were you planning to do? Poison the garden?"

Johannes forced himself to get up. He was going to go outside and feed his birds. "You never understood farming," he muttered as he headed for the door. "Didn't want to. As much as I tried to explain."

Susanna turned around, blocking his way. "Of course I understand farming, Dad." He wished he'd kept quiet. "It's all about high yields and fuck the rest, isn't it?" She punctuated her outburst by throwing things indiscriminately into the box. "Fuck the water table! Fuck the soil! And fuck the earth, while we're at it."

All that swearing - she must have learnt it at boarding school. Kate and he never spoke like that.

"That's exactly why I became an environmentalist, Dad - to try to protect nature from farmers like you."

The dust from the boxes was making him sneeze so he started to walk towards the birdbath. Susanna followed him into the blinding sunlight. He turned on the hosepipe.

"I used to help your mother in the garden." It came out so pathetic.

"Help? Why was Mom always devastated after you 'helped' her? One day she'd be showing me how beautifully the branches of the ziziphus were arching over the path and the next moment you'd gone and pruned and mutilated the tree!"

"She let things go wild. One couldn't walk along those paths without having to bend over or get hit in the face by thorns."

Susanna wiped her forehead with her sleeve. "You never did understand what Mom was trying to do in her garden." She was close to tears. "Or maybe you were jealous of her?"

Johannes pointed at the box full of bottles. "I don't want you to throw away my things without asking me!"

"You were jealous of all the things that made her happy." Her voice was shrill now. "Because you are just such a bloody miserable person."

"That's not true." It was too hot out here, he had to get inside. Johannes closed the tap and walked up the stairs to the veranda as fast as he could manage. She followed him closely.

"I loved Kate," he heard himself saying.

"Then how did you show it?"

"You don't have to speak so loud. Everyone on the path can hear you."

She raised her voice defiantly. "We used to dread it when you came home, Mom and I. All that misery you brought into the house."

They reached the veranda and Susanna took off the yellow rubber gloves and lit a cigarette. Her hands were shaking. Johannes sat down heavily on his rocking chair catching his breath.

"You could never go along with anything Mom and I wanted."

He was rocking harder and harder. "You don't understand everything, you know," he said. "You don't know what it was like." His mouth was dry. "I loved Anna."

Susanna looked at him. "What does Auntie Anna have to do with all of this?"

"I meant Kate, I loved Kate." His heart was beating fast now.

Susanna finished her cigarette and got up to go inside.

He didn't seem to be able to breathe that well. He could hear her rummaging about in her room. There was nothing he could do about it now. She just had to do what she had to do.

When Susanna came out of the house, she had changed into a colourful African skirt that sat too tightly around her hips. She was carrying a briefcase and a camera.

"Won't you open the gate for me?" She held out the bunch of keys towards him. "I can't cope with this. I need to go for a drive.

See if I can organise some interviews in Kareepan."

Johannes followed her down the stairs and opened the big gate.

"I was never any good with words," he tried again.

Advent at Evening Star

As soon as I hear the Dodge coming up our hill I run to Thambulo's house because I don't feel like seeing Uncle Els. Asta is very happy to visit Tshamato and they go off sniffing and scratching around the yard, their tails wagging as they chase a mouse in the grass. It's still early and the only people up are Thambulo's sister, Masindi, and another woman I haven't seen before who's wearing a red salampore. VhoSarah is already at our house boiling water for the pig they are going to slaughter later. Masindi and her friend are making porridge in the kitchen hut so I sit down and watch them.

"Aren't you going to khotha to us?" Masindi teases me.

Someone is coughing in the sleeping hut. Masindi tells me that it's her friend's mother. They've brought her here so that Mutti can give her some medicine and pray for her.

"When you go home, you must tell the Vhafunzi's wife that she must come here after church," Masindi's friend says, pointing at the sleeping hut.

After a while Mukegulu comes out of her hut.

"Ndaa!" I greet her. She is carrying Masindi's baby.

"Aah!" she replies.

"Where is Thambulo?"

'He's still sleeping.'

As Mukegulu passes me a plate of hot porridge with sour milk, Anna comes running from the house. She quickly kneels down in front of Mukegulu to greet her.

"You see, Hannes," says Masindi "even your little sister knows how to greet the elders."

"You have to come and help Uncle Els and Mutti with the pig, Hannes." Anna is out of breath. "They want to slaughter it before church."

I don't feel like going. After church Missionary Els is taking us with him to Evening Star for a few days. He and Mutti are going to fill in the school requisition forms for the Department of Education together because Mutti doesn't understand English so well.

"Why can't we go in our car?" I asked this morning.

"I'm grateful that Uncle Els has offered to fetch us," Mutti said.

Anna doesn't want to go either, but Mutti pointed out that it is the first of Advent and that it would be nice to be among Germans.

"And," Mutti added, "I need a break from Wittenberg."

When I get to the house Uncle Els is standing on the kitchen veranda in his clean white overcoat, his shotgun is leaning against the frangipani tree. He is sharpening the big slaughter knife. I go and shake his hand, it feels rough and dry.

"And have you been a good boy?" asks Uncle Els. He always speaks so slowly, as if he's afraid of losing some words.

Mutti reassures him that I am very helpful. "Just sometimes he forgets to speak German."

The pig is screaming as Sipho and Godwill drag it up the hill towards the house. Uncle Els tugs at his short red beard and wipes his hands on his overcoat. He is wearing his suit pants and shirt underneath because he is going to conduct the service today.

It's a young pig from the July litter. It screams so loud that Anna and I have to close our ears and it struggles as Sipho and Godwill tie it to the frangipani tree. Anna and I stand inside the kitchen door so we can't see. VhoSarah goes outside to help hold down the pig and it calms down.

When the shotgun goes off, I close my eyes.

They load the body onto a plank and carry it into the slaughter room. I want to go and look for Asta, but Mutti sees me and calls me back.

"Go and fetch another bucket of hot water from the bathing drum, Hannes."

Mukegulu also arrives to help.

It is dark in the slaughter room. All I can see is the split-open rump of the pig hanging on the hook. The head and hams are already soaking in a salt brine in the tin bath. Mukegulu and VhoSarah collect the intestines for washing. Tomorrow, when we are away, they will make sausages and when we come back, Mutti will put them in the smoker. Mutti asks me to wrap the ribs in muslin cloths. She says we are going to take those with us to Evening Star.

Uncle Els wipes the big knife with surgical spirits. It's because pigs have worms, he tells me. Mutti goes and makes him a strong cup of coffee.

When the first church bell rings Anna and I quickly close all the windows and call the chicken into the storeroom because of the monkeys.

Today we can't sit with Thambulo and Mukegulu and VhoSarah, we have to sit in the front pew with Mutti and the Evangelists because Uncle Els is holding the service. During the last verse of the hymn he slowly climbs up onto the pulpit. It's going to be a long slow sermon.

After lunch Mukegulu and VhoSarah help us pack the black Dodge. Anna and I sit in the back and Willie is lucky because he can sit in front on Mutti's lap. We wave goodbye and I don't know why but I'm feeling a bit sad. Then I remember about the sick woman in the mudi and wonder if I should tell Mutti about it now, but it's too late. We are already driving past Old Wittenberg.

"Do you think there is a matukwane living there?" I ask Anna.

"Where do you hear such nonsense?" Uncle Els has got very good ears. "You children must not listen to such superstitious nonsense."

It's hot in the car and Anna and I open our windows. Then we close them and open them again. Mutti tells us to stop that immediately, so we leave the windows as they are and let the wind blow through our hair. Anna's hair comes loose and blows into my face. I take a thick strand and stretch it across my eyes so that I can look at the sun, like tropical protection glasses. Anna laughs.

Missionary Els turns around and nearly drives off the road. He tells us to close the windows immediately and keep quiet because he can't hear what our Mutti is saying.

She's telling him about the mission farm.

"And you know, Rolf, we've hardly got any young men left living on the farm. They're all working on the mines. And those that are here just don't show me any respect," Mutti says. "They refuse to help with anything."

Uncle Els shakes his head and says, "The heathens are and will always be stubborn and lazy people."

"But these are not heathens," Mutti explains. "These are our people, they're Christians."

"If they don't want to work, Elisabeth, you have every right to kick them off the mission land."

"As soon as I show any softness, they abuse it. Just the other day I lent our plough to old Ephraim's son and now he doesn't want to return it. I have asked him over and over again to please bring it back." She sighs.

We are nearly out of the forest and I wonder whether Masindi's friend's mother is going to die.

Uncle Els is telling Mutti about the bottlestore that the Scottish trader has opened near Evening Star. "I keep telling Mr McCann that you can't sell drink to the heathens. It destroys them."

Luckily there hasn't been so much rain this spring and the Mbwedi River is low. Once when Willie was very sick, Mutti had to ask Maharaj to take her to the clinic and when they crossed the river it was so full that Maharaj had to take off the fan belt and cover the engine with a mealie-meal bag to keep it dry.

Anna and I open the windows again so that we can hang out of the car to watch the tyres go over the rocks of the shallow riverbed.

"I don't know what to do anymore," Mutti continues. "I'm afraid that if I get too strict the young men will come and do something to us. You never know with the natives."

It's a long way to Evening Star and everything looks very different. There's lots of dry grass with a few thorn trees around. We stop twice on the way so that Uncle Els can go and wee in the bushes. When the sun is already far to the west, we finally get to Evening Star. A boy opens the gate and follows us, running behind the car. As soon as we stop at the building, he opens the car doors for us and carries all our bags. When Mutti reaches for her bag, Uncle Els chides her.

"You need to learn to let others do the work sometimes, Elisabeth," he pats her on her arm with his dry hand.

As we start walking towards the veranda, two big black dogs come charging out of the house, snarling and barking. We stand still. They have sharp pointy ears and big teeth.

"Wilfried, Conrad!" Uncle Els shouts. "Come and call these dogs of yours."

Uncle Els hits the bigger one on the snout with his umbrella. It yelps and they slink off into the garden.

"I apologise for that." Uncle Els says. "But we need good guard dogs here."

The house at Evening Star is much smaller and darker than ours. Uncle Els leads us through the lounge with its many doors and calls his sons again. "Wilfried, Conrad! Where are you?"

There are papers and hats and tools lying everywhere on the chairs and tables and Uncle Els apologises that his house is so untidy.

"You're all going to sleep in the main bedroom," Uncle Els declares. "Since Friedhild left us I have taken to sleeping on the daybed in my study."

"Where did Auntie Friedhild go?" asks Anna. "Mutti said she was dead."

Mutti gives Anna a funny look.

"You are quite right, my child." Uncle Els smiles. "I have no doubt that your Auntie Friedhild has gone to heaven."

The room where we are going to sleep smells of old feathers and soil. It's almost completely filled with a big wooden bed covered with a faded quilt and in the corner is a crib for Willie to sleep in. Above it is a picture of Jesus reaching over an abyss towards a bleating lamb that has got lost and fallen onto a rocky ledge. A vulture circles the sky above it.

"We're going to have a lot of fun all sleeping in this big bed together," Mutti announces as she pulls up the sachet window to let in some air. "Thank you Rolf."

She puts Willie down on the bed and, when Uncle Els leaves, Anna and I jump onto it as well. Mutti pours water into the basin on the washstand and takes off Willie's nappy. Anna and I hold our noses and try not to giggle too much. Then Anna points to the long hippo-hide whip standing in the corner next to the cupboard and we giggle some more.

When Willie is nice and clean again we all go into the lounge. Wilfried and Conrad are sitting on the sofa and pretend that they haven't seen us. The big black dogs are sitting at their feet. When Mutti goes up to the boys to greet them, the dogs growl.

Wilfried looks a lot like Auntie Friedhild whose portrait hangs above the piano. He has spiky hair and the same fierce eyebrows that meet between the eyes. Mutti told us that Auntie Friedhild died long ago already but that Uncle Els feels that he has to wait a few years before he can start looking for a new wife.

"Especially now that there is a war, there is very little chance that Uncle Rolf will be getting a wife sent from Germany soon," Mutti told us.

The boys shake Mutti's hand without getting up. Conrad is younger than Wilfried. They both go to an Afrikaans boarding school in Pretoria. Mutti says that when I'm old enough she is going to send me there too.

She leaves Anna and me standing in the lounge and goes looking for a bucket to put Willie's dirty nappy into. When she comes back she pushes some papers and clothes off a big easy chair and sits down with Willie on her lap. Anna and I squeeze in next to her. It's almost dark in the room and Mutti looks about nervously. Uncle Els doesn't have that many books, not like we have at home - just a big bookcase with glass doors behind which stands a neat row of black bibles and hymnbooks.

Finally Uncle Els arrives. "Have you greeted our visitors yet?" He ruffles Wilfried's hair and the boys nod their heads.

"You must excuse the boys. They haven't had a mother to teach them manners," Uncle Els says.

Then suddenly he turns around and calls: "Rebecca! Rebecca!"

Anna jumps with fright. She's been staring at Auntie Friedhild's photograph. Two women, dressed in large German print uniforms and white pinafores come running out of the kitchen.

"Look how late it is already!" Uncle Els scolds them. "And the lamps aren't even lit yet."

"Sorry, Moruti," they say and bow their heads and quickly run back into the kitchen.

For supper we eat pork ribs and bread with jam but I'm not so hungry. Wilfried and Conrad don't say much at table. They just giggle when Uncle Els tells Anna and me to take our elbows off the table. His beard is full of pork fat and he keeps wiping at it. When the women come to take away the plates, the boys say something to each other in Afrikaans and laugh.

After supper Mutti feeds Willie and puts him into the crib next to our bed and we all go through to the lounge where Mutti clears the coffee table to make space for the Advent wreath that she brought for the Els'. Anna and I picked the cypress branches yesterday and helped her. We also made one for our lounge. When Anna and I squeeze into the chair with Mutti again, she gets up to light the first of the four thick red Advent candles on the wreath.

"I think you two should find your own chair to sit on," Mutti whispers to us.

I point to the dogs lying on the carpet snoring and Mutti lets us stay in the chair with her.

Uncle Els goes to the cupboard and pours a thick green drink into four tiny glasses. He says that his boys are already allowed to drink because they have been confirmed. Mutti has put out the big Advent plate full of cookies we baked and the pecan nuts and dried fruit. As soon as the adults aren't looking, the boys grab a handful and stuff them into their mouths.

Uncle Els remembers that he meant to go and fetch some sheet music from his study for us to sing from.

"Come with me Elisabeth, then you can choose which arrangements you like."

As soon as they go outside the boys jump up again and grab Christmas cookies and dried mangoes but Anna and I stay in our chair. The light from the lamps is jumpy.

A bat flies in through the front door and Wilfried fetches a tennis racket and chases it around the room. Finally he swats at it and brings it down hard. He takes it by the wing tip and dangles it right in front of Anna's face. It's still breathing, its square mouth showing its fangs and there's blood dripping from its nose.

"Here's a bat for the Venda girl," Wilfried sniggers. "You can use it to make your peepee go longer."

Anna looks at the bat, then at Wilfried and straightens herself in the chair. "My father's horse," she says confidently, "was killed by a black mamba."

Wilfried and Conrad laugh and then Wilfried throws the bat out into the night and grabs some more cookies.

When Mutti and Uncle Els come back Mutti clears the piano stool and settles herself down in front of the keys.

"The children have already eaten far too many Advent cookies,"

Uncle Els says admonishingly. "I think, Elisabeth, we will have to pack them away."

Mutti doesn't seem to hear him and starts to play the piano. "Come stand behind me, children." She beckons us. "Like we do at home."

She plays a few opening bars and then she starts to sing in her high, sweet voice: *'Macht hoch die Tűr, die Tor macht weit.'*

Anna and I join in. The boys sit back in the sofa and fold their arms while Uncle Els fumbles his way through the descant on his recorder.

When we have sung all five verses Mutti sighs and then she wipes her eyes.

I also miss Father tonight.

12.

She checked her handbag for her sunglasses and cell phone and started the car. It was stupid to think that she and Dad could spend more than twenty-four hours together without all the old stuff coming up again. Besides it was fucking hot in this god-forsaken place. She turned on the air conditioner. She really couldn't help him; he would just have to die a lonely old man.

She tried to relax into the soft leather seats of the car as she drove with the dust billowing up behind her. She would go and book herself into the B&B in Stillefontein right away. The food wasn't up to scratch, but at least there was the swimming pool and she could visit Dad and leave just as and when it suited her. She could get all the interviews done in the next few weeks. After that maybe she could even find a cottage at the sea and write up the research proposal.

A large herd of cattle was being led across the road. They were confused and skittish, creating a large cloud of dust. Probably Jooste's herd. It wasn't a good idea to let them graze when the veld was this decimated, it could easily get bankrotbos started, and then you could forget that piece of veld for at least the next twenty years.

When she reached the main road, Susanna changed her mind and turned left towards Kareepan. She could always book into the B&B later. She felt like getting going, at least set up some interviews for this week.

Shortly before Kareepan, the tar road turned into a rutted dirt road again and she drove towards the tin shacks. There was no one at the communal tap, only a few goats rooting around in the dust. The water had probably dried up. A man on a horse cart carrying firewood waved at her. He must have travelled far - the koppies around here were mostly stripped of trees already. The horse was thin and scraggly and probably had saddle sores. Three children were playing next to the road, a thin dog by their side. Susanna smiled and waved at them.

A soft bang and a thud: "Shit!"

She got out and walked around the car. The back left tyre was flat. The children ran towards her whooping and laughing, their dog wagged its tail. She wished she could speak Zulu or Sotho. People emerged from their shacks and the man on the horse cart drew up slowly. He shook his head in commiseration.

"Puncture," he said as he jumped off the cart. "It always happens on this road." He whistled through his teeth. "Doesn't happen much with these big cars though."

She smiled at him and went to open the boot to look for the spare tire and the jack. She had never used them before, never even read the instructions. Before she could stop him, the man lifted out the spare tyre and unfolded the jack.

"The roads are terrible," he said. "This government, eish!"

It was almost unbearably hot outside and the flies were seeking out her face.

"Do you know where I can find some of the community leaders?"

The man loosened the nuts of the tyre before lying down on the road to inspect the underside of her car for a place to fit the jack.

"I want to do some research here. About the environmental impact of rural townships."

"The councillor lives in that big blue house over there." He got up and slowly and expertly jacked up the car.

More people gathered around them, men coming to give advice, two young girls with babies on their backs. The girls inspect her briefcase. "It's nice," one of them said.

Susanna took out her cell phone and put the bag on the back seat.

"Where are you from?" asked the other girl.

"I'm from Johannesburg," she replied, wishing she didn't feel so nervous.

"That's far." They looked impressed. "Can you take us with you?"

"I'm working here at the moment." She pointed at the township and the koppies.

They laughed incredulously. Suddenly a tall young man walked towards them, parting the crowd. He was wearing tight jeans and a short tank top revealing a flat, muscular belly adorned with an ornate fake ruby belly ring.

"Hi sweetie," his voice like honey through his scowl.

"No man, S'bu," someone grumbled. "Leave her alone. She's lost."

She faced him. "Good morning. What do you want?"

"So you're lost?"

"No, I'm not lost. I just have a puncture." She must not lose her temper.

"Ag shame, sweetie." The sarcasm was clear. The crowd thinned out.

Her phone rang. It was Althea. Relieved, Susanna walked to the front of the car and answered it. The young man followed her.

"You won't believe it, I've just driven into the township outside Stillefontein to set up interviews and now I've got a puncture."

She could feel the young man watching her. "I had a fight with my dad this morning. I'm going to set myself up at the local bed and breakfast for a while. I'll e-mail you from there."

Althea was starting to give her advice about formulating the proposal when, out of the corner of her eye, Susanna noticed that the man was holding a gun, dangling it from his fingers like a cowboy. He didn't like to be ignored, it seemed.

"I've got to go," she said.

"Aah, I see. You are one of those clever people," the man said. "I always wanted to have a clever girlfriend." She noticed that the fingernails on his left hand were painted pink. "And one with a nice car and cell phone."

She could feel her skin burning in the sun. The car was being lowered onto the ground again. The horse and cart man was standing next to her.

"Don't, S'bu," the man said angrily. "Don't make trouble."

"Don't worry, Pappie. I just asked this bitch whether she'll be my girlfriend." He smiled.

Never resist they say. Never resist.

"But it seems she isn't interested. So at least you can give me that phone, bitch."

He'd watched far too much TV. "You think you can intimidate

everyone, don't you?" she hissed.

"Ag shame, Miesies." He lifted the gun towards her.

It didn't feel real. "Put that gun away."

"You better do what he says," said the man next to her. "This one's trouble."

The young man grinned. "You hear what Pappie here says."

"First put that gun away," she couldn't help answering.

He tucked the gun into the back of his jeans and she handed him the phone. She could smell him now, sweet alcoholic aftershave. Maybe he was drunk. He walked away slowly.

People started crowding around her.

"Where is the police station?" The hysteria again, rising from her belly.

"It won't help. He's not from here."

"Leave her now," an elderly woman with a leopard print headscarf said and took hold of Susanna's arm. "Come, have some sweet tea, Mammie."

"Don't worry." Susanna could hardly speak. "I'll be all right. I need to get to the councillor's office."

"Have some tea first."

"Thank you, no, I'm really fine."

She got into the car and started it. Maybe she should give the man who had helped her some money. She reached for her bag and then changed her mind and wound down the window. He was about to climb back onto his cart again.

"Thank you so much," she said, her voice dry and thin.

"I'm so sorry," he replied.

She drove off, steadying her hands on the steering wheel. The children with the dog were waving at her in the rear-view mirror and she tried to slow down, not to make too much dust for them. But then she sped up again - she had to get out of Kareepan as quickly as possible.

Thambulo and I see the Pythonman

Asta is so happy to see us when we came back from Evening Star that she even follows me to the toilet and sits outside the door waiting. But at night I can't fall asleep because I'm worried about the sick woman at the mudi I had forgotten to tell Mutti about, and about Thambulo going home for the Christmas holidays before I can tell him all about our visit and show him the pocket knife that Conrad gave me.

As soon as I hear Mukegulu and VhoSarah coming into the kitchen in the morning, I get dressed and go look for them.

"Has Thambulo gone home for Christmas yet?"

Mukegulu and VhoSarah laugh at me. "Aren't you going to greet us, our son?"

I quickly kneel to khotha.

"He hasn't gone away," Mukegulu reassures me.

I finish my breakfast quickly and run to the mudi with Asta. I find Thambulo lying in the sleeping hut on his mat staring at the ceiling.

"Are you sick, Thambulo?" I ask.

He shakes his head.

I tell him about Evening Star which doesn't have any forests or mountains and only a few thorn trees and about Wilfried and Conrad who are going to get hunting rifles for Christmas so that they can shoot wild dogs and monkeys for pocket money. And then I show him my pocketknife. But I can see that Thambulo's not really listening.

"Are you cross with me, Thambulo?"

"No. I'm not allowed to go home to Ntshelele this Christmas," he sighs. "Mukegulu got a letter yesterday. My oldest brother has come back from the mines because he is sick. Now my other brother has gone to Johannesburg to look for a job. They say it's better if I stay here."

He looks so sad and I wonder how I can cheer him up.

"They promised I could go home."

"I know."

"And I wanted to get my things."

He's getting even sadder and I don't want Thambulo to cry so I show him my handstands that I practised at Evening Star. But he isn't really interested.

"Why don't we go to Old Wittenberg and see what's in the house?" I say excitedly.

"Your mother won't allow it."

"I don't care. I'm big now."

"But what if we disturb the spirits? I've got enough bad luck already."

"Missionary Els says that that's all heathen superstition."

Thambulo hesitates but then he gets up and puts on his shorts and combs his hair.

We go outside, eat a bit of muladza and then walk down to the forest path. Asta and Tshiamo follow us. It's a nice hot day and I'm happy we are walking in the cool forest and I can't stop talking. I don't care whether Mutti is looking for me or whether she tells Father or Uncle Els or anyone.

As soon as the collapsed walls of the old house appear, Thambulo lifts his finger to his mouth and I keep quiet. Asta's hair starts to rise on her back and she and Tshiamo turn around and run off back home. I try to call her but she doesn't listen.

The brambles are getting thicker and we have to beat them aside with our sticks. A pair of pigeons fly up heavily. My heart beats faster. Mutti told me that the windows and doors of Old Wittenberg were taken out and used to build Evangelist David's house on the other side of the church and that he nearly refused to move in because it would bring bad luck. Missionary Bester had to convince him. A yellow rambling rose hangs over the front door, almost covering the entrance.

As we approach the doorway, a genet runs past us hissing, fleeing into the bush.

"It's a witch," Thambulo whispers.

The wind makes funny noises in the chimney. There's a rusty cooking pot on the floor of the kitchen. We slowly make our way across the broken floorboards to the main room. I peek into the old bedroom. A lizard scurries over the wall and hides behind a scrap of pale blue wallpaper.

"Can you feel it?" Thambulo says.

"What?"

Thambulo is shivering and fat drops of sweat collect on his forehead.

"Look there." He points to a hollow in the floor in the far corner.

I can't see anything because it's dark in here.

"I think it's the Pythonman." Thambulo's lips hardly move.

I look hard. And then I can see something move.

We run. We run out of the front door as fast as our legs will carry us. And we keep on running, back up the path, through the brambles and bushes, all the way up. Only once we can't see the old house anymore do we stop to catch our breath.

Thambulo looks at me, panting. "I didn't think it would be so big!"

"Neither did I!"

Thambulo wipes his forehead and we collapse onto the ground. "Did you see its head? It had a man's head." He looks at me and starts to laugh. "You looked so scared!"

Our arms and legs are full of scratches.

"You too!"

"I've never had such a fright in my life!" Thambulo starts to laugh again.

"What was it?"

"The Pythonman. The one that protects the chiefs' graves."

Once we have caught our breath and recovered, Thambulo pulls me up and we continue walking along the path again. Soon I realise that everything looks unfamiliar.

"Do you know where we are, Thambulo?"

"We're going to the waterfall," he explains.

"Yes," I say. I feel happy and light again. "Let's go for a swim."

I run ahead for a while, but then the path is steep and the forest gets thicker. Up here you can't even hear any cowbells. Just as my legs are getting tired and I'm starting to wonder if we'll ever get to the waterfall, we scramble over a big rock and there it is, right in front of us - a big bright waterfall gushing into a perfect pool.

Thambulo takes off all his clothes and quickly dives into the water. Silver droplets run through his hair and down his face and he smiles at me. Ferns and purple and white star flowers grow among the rocks all around the waterfall.

"Is it cold?"

Thambulo gestures for me to jump in and vanishes under the water again. He rolls his body like an otter, occasionally coming up for air only to vanish deeper and longer. For a moment I worry but then he comes up holding something in his hand.

"Look what I found."

I go closer and he splashes me with water. "Got you!" he shouts and dives under the water.

I take my clothes off, carefully folding them and hanging them over a dead branch full of bearded lichen. The stones hurt my feet, but before Thambulo can splash me again I jump into the icy water and quickly find a place where I can stand because I haven't learnt to swim properly yet. My body looks blue and white under the water, like a skinned goat. Thambulo laughs and goes right under the waterfall and lets the spray fall on his head. I join him. The spray is hard and it stings my face. Something brushes against my legs and I scream.

"It's the water spirit," Thambulo mocks me. "Zwidutwane wants to come and live inside you."

And then he too starts to scream. We scream hard and long against the gushing water. We scream and scream till our voices are hoarse and we laugh and hug each other.

Thambulo gets out of the water and I follow him. We go and lie on our tummies on the hot rocks.

"I'm hungry," Thambulo says dreamily. "I wish we could catch some nice fat pigeons and roast them."

The sun shines on our cold bodies and I fall asleep.

13

The midday heat shimmered over everything and as soon as she reached the tar road, Susanna stopped to light a cigarette. Shit, shit, shit! She pounded the steering wheel with her fists. The bastard! Her cell phone of all things. She had to try and calm down, decide what to do next.

Finding an old farm track that seemed to lead up to the koppie, she drove across the cattle grid and through a broken gate. As she reached the top she parked her car next to a thin bush that offered no shade. At least she had brought a bottle of water.

Susanna put out her cigarette and walked up along the ridge. After a while she crossed a little farm road and by the time she reached the top of the koppie, sweat was running down her back. Below she could see the grove of sweet-thorns from yesterday, and the ancient stonewall circles protecting the trees from fire. She stumbled down the rocky slope. A flock of guinea fowl screeched out of the trees.

When she reached the ruins she sat down on a rock under a tree and drank greedily from the water bottle. The sky stretched pale over the farmlands ahead. She was shaking now. A fucking gun. He had pointed a fucking gun at her. She lit another cigarette.

A little rainbow skink crawled out of the crevice eying her curiously. All those phone numbers! She'd have to go and get her diary from Dad's house. The lizard circled her boot and vanished. She couldn't stay long, she had to find a cell phone shop in Stillefontein and call the service provider. Cancel the SIM card. There was bound to be a dingy little electronics shop there somewhere where she could buy a new phone.

It was all such a mess, first the fight with Dad and now this.

Where were the buck? She wanted to see the rheebuck.

Again she could feel her anger rising. Who the fuck did he think he was? She should go back immediately and report him to the police. But first she wanted to sit here a while longer and wait for the buck to come back. Where were they? They had come so suddenly yesterday, crashing through the thicket - a male and a female. When they saw her they had stopped and looked at her, ready to run away again.

"Just stay a bit," she had pleaded. The male flicked his coat, watching her. And then the female had lowered her head and started grazing. Every movement so careful. "Stay," she had willed them. But then, as if reading her thoughts, the male had pricked up his ears, gave a piercing whistle and ran off. The female had looked at her once more and then followed him.

She was about to get up when, from the corner of her eye, Susanna saw a snake crawling out of the same crevice that the skink had vanished into. She sat dead still, feeling her heart beat in her ears. It was a thin brown one, probably a harmless Bush Snake, but still. It headed straight for her boot. She held her breath. Just don't move.

It seemed so curious, stopping right next to her foot, flickering its tongue, looking at her through the narrow slits of its eyes. It slid onto her boot watching her, hesitating. She could feel the tension drain from her body.

"Hey little thing," she whispered. "A man just held a gun in my face." She closed her eyes and released her breath, feeling the slight weight of the snake on her foot. The cicadas screeched. Heavy sobs were building up in her chest and she quickly opened her eyes to stop them. The snake was still there, looking at her, basking in the sun. They sat for a while, but then the old restlessness shot through her. It was madness to sit there with a snake on her foot. She got up quickly and kicked it off. The snake landed against the rock and lay there. Oh shit! Now she'd probably gone and killed it.

Susanna walked up the steep slope towards the car as fast as she could.

"You stupid woman," she chided herself. "It trusted you."

In the **orchard**

Mutti and Willie have gone to Kimberley to visit Father, but Anna and I aren't allowed to go because we are too old now. It's Father's fourth Christmas in Andalusia already, so we made him a book of stories about all that happens at Wittenberg with drawings. Anna and I also had to go to the studio in Louis Trichardt to have a photograph taken so that Father can see what we look like. The man at the studio had a monkey on a chain in front of his house.

Mutti says that nowadays they have a proper visiting room at Andalusia, where the men sit on the one side of a long table and their visitors sit on the other. But still, Mutti is always so sad when she comes back and sometimes she gets sick.

The last two times when Mutti visited Father, Anna and I had to stay at the Els'. This year we are lucky because Miss Talbot has offered to come and stay with us. Miss Talbot is alright. She doesn't like being outside much and spends a lot of time reading in her room. At least she lets us be with our friends and I can go hunting with Thambulo and his friends whenever I want to.

"As long as you practise your English on each other," she says, and we know she's just pretending to be strict.

Today Mukegulu has asked Thambulo and I to go to the orchard to pick avocados before the monkeys get them. We're going to pack them into crates and store them in the slaughter room because it's nice and cool in there and they will last longer.

I climb right to the top of the trees and pick the fruit while Thambulo stands on the ground, ready to catch the avocados. They are as large as ostrich eggs and sometimes they hurt your fingers when you catch them. We laugh a lot, especially when an avocado crashes down by accident and splatters into a buttery pulp against the branches, or when Thambulo manages to catch one by flinging himself onto the ground after it. Mukegulu says sometimes we are just like two girls, giggling all the time like that.

It's hot today and I can see the girls sitting nearby, eating mangoes off the trees. They're always talking and whispering, and sometimes practicing dance steps. Chief Ravhura's mudi isn't very far from us and lately the people have been singing and dancing up there a lot. Whenever she has a chance, Noria goes and watches the tshigombela team practise their steps, then she comes back and teaches Anna.

When we have filled three crates with avocados, Thambulo and I decide to creep up on the girls and give them a fright. I'm just about to jump out and enjoy their shrieks when Thambulo signals for me to be quiet.

"Listen," he whispers.

"My sister is starting to grow hair down there," Noria says, pointing a hairy mango pip to where her legs meet.

"That's terrible," Anna says. "Does she have to go to the clinic?"

"No, silly," laughs Noria. "Every girl gets hair down there. It's when you get ready for the red to come."

"What's that?"

"When you bleed so that you can make children and go to vhusha."

Anna looks amazed. "I hurt myself all the time but Mutti says I'm too small to have children."

"But you don't bleed in your underpants."

I look at Thambulo. I've never heard such rubbish in my life before, but he just smiles.

"As soon as the first red comes down you have to tell your mother and she will call the chief's wife and you have to lie in cold water the whole day so you can shed your skin."

I shiver. All I had heard about vhusha is that Missionary Els says that the Vhavenda do terrible things to their girls during the initiation rites.

"My sister says you have to walk to the road without any clothes on and then, when you see the boys you have to ask them for snuff so you can give it to your mothers."

"With no clothes on?" Anna is shocked.

"Some of the girls in my class go in the morning to pull their peepee with powder they make from bat wings."

Anna holds her hands in front of her mouth in surprise. "I thought Wilfried was lying to me."

I can feel my penis getting thick. It's been doing that a lot lately. Thambulo says his does it all the time also and that it is a good thing because it means you are a man. Still, I don't like it when it happens, especially when there are people around.

"My mother says my father will probably allow me to go to vhusha because he can't stop that. But domba we are not allowed." Noria sighs.

Thambulo can't hold himself back any more. He crashes out of our hiding place. "In Ntshelele I went to domba every time."

I wish he hadn't. I wanted to hear more of what the girls have to say and I don't want them to see the thing in my pants and tease me.

Noria is angry. "You know boys aren't allowed to listen to girls when we talk quietly together."

Thambulo looks around for support so I have to come out from behind the litchi tree as well. I sit down immediately next to the girls, glad that they haven't noticed anything.

"In Masindi's year there were over a hundred girls graduating."

"Masindi is lucky," says Noria. "My father wouldn't even let us go to watch. My mother argues with him all the time. She says her daughters won't find a good man if they don't know the ways of a woman."

"You've never seen so many people coming from all over." Thambulo gathers the people from right around us with his arms. "There's dancing day and night and so much food and more and more people come."

"They teach you many things at the domba," Noria says.

Anna jumps up. "Let's dance domba."

The others jump up and Thambulo is the leader and Noria and Anna fall in behind him. They hold onto each other's elbows and Thambulo slowly steers them in a circle around the tree, their arms against their bodies moving in waves, like the ripple of a python as it moves itself along the ground.

"Come Hannes," Anna shouts. "Come dance with us."

I shake my head and then Anna points at my pants, "Look, Hannes has a carrot in his shorts!"

I try to cover it but they're dancing around me now, laughing.

"Hannes is getting ready to grind the corn!" Thambulo says.

"It's not a corn grinder, it's a carrot!" chirps Anna.

"And what do you know?" I turn on Anna.

"Wilfried showed me his." She looks at me defiantly. "He said he wanted to show me what a man looks like."

"And did you look?"

"Yes and I told him it looked exactly like an ugly old carrot. So he told me it's what women want. So I asked him what women want such an ugly peepee for and he said, "Because they do, they can't help themselves'."

We all laugh at Wilfried's stupidity, and Thambulo, Noria and Anna carry on dancing the domba, winding their way through the orchard.

Then Miss Talbot calls us to come inside and we take the avos down to the slaughterhouse and say goodbye to Noria and Thambulo.

When Anna and I get inside VhoSarah and Mukegulu have already lit the lamps in the kitchen for the evening prayers. Miss Talbot struggles through a passage from the Tshivenda Bible.

Tonight VhoSarah looks so beautiful in the lamplight.

Once she is done Miss Talbot says, "Tomorrow you can read from the Bible for us, Hannes." She says this every evening but the next day she seems to forget again. But at least she lets Mukegulu pray because she says she doesn't know how to do that.

Mukegulu prays for Mutti and Father and for Willie who are far away. She prays for our family in Germany and for Miss Talbot's family who live in Scotland. She prays for Thambulo's father and mother who are lost somewhere in Johannesburg, and for all the people at her home in Nshelele. She prays for VhoSarah's family that lives far away too. Just as she is about to say Amen, Anna reminds her not to forget Noria's family.

Then we sing the hymn. VhoSarah's voice is low and soft. One day when I finish school, I want to marry her.

14

He took forever to open the gate. His hands were shaking badly - all that coffee he is drinking couldn't be good for him. He'd probably been sitting on the veranda all day rocking as if his life depended on it. If he wasn't careful, he'd fall right through those floorboards one day.

"Leave the gate open," Susanna said as she drove past him, "I have to leave again just now, I've come to pack my things."

She got out of the car and quickly walked up the stairs into the house. Everything was still in a mess with the rubbish bags lying around and the kitchen in disarray, but there was no way she could stay and tidy up now.

Susanna threw her things into her bags. As soon as she had a phone again, she would call Grace and ask her to pop in tomorrow. She should come in at least twice a week. Susanna would pay her well and sooner or later he would get used to it. She lifted the bags off the bed and started to strip off the sheets. She could feel him watching her from the door, sweaty and out of breath. He really wasn't looking well.

"Are you okay, Dad?"

He didn't seem to hear her. Knowing him, he probably didn't want to. She bent over to straighten the faded old bedspread and stubbed her toe against Grandfather's old kist.

"Ouch!"

"I wanted to speak to you about that old kist," he said.

"Not now Dad," her voice shriller than she intended. "Let's talk about it some other time."

"I want you to take it and decide what to do with the things."

"I'm in a hurry Dad."

"Don't you at least want a cup of coffee before you go?" he added.

"No thanks, Dad." She lifted the heavy bags and squeezed past him.

"You have to be patient with me," he said. "I'm clumsy. I don't know how to be with people. I never did. It's from growing up on a mission station. Willie says he has the same problem."

"It's not just you, Dad." She could feel herself soften. "It's me. I'm in a mess. I need to be alone for a bit."

He followed her down the stairs and to the car. She threw the bags into the back and slammed the boot closed.

"I'm sorry," he said.

She tried hugging him, but he was all bones and elbows so she opened the door, ready to jump into the car. As long as he didn't start crying now.

"I'll come and see you," she said. "As soon as I feel better."

"Will you write down your phone number for me again? I don't know where I put it."

"My phone was stolen."

He looked shocked. "When?"

"Just now. In Kareepan."

Johannes shook his head. "One has to be so careful nowadays."

He was about to touch her, but she quickly put on her sunglasses and jumped up onto the seat and looked in her handbag to see if she had forgotten anything.

"I tried to love her."

He looked so pathetic. She had no energy for all this now.

"Bye Dad," she tried to sound cheerful. "I just need to sort out a few things."

Susanna started the car and slowly reversed out of the yard. She could see him in the rear view mirror looking like a sad old bird.

As she passed the old car wreck there was a sudden wind that blew up a cloud of dust and debris across the road. Before she turned the corner she glanced over her shoulder one more time. He was standing there at the gate, struggling with the lock. She hoped he would be okay. Maybe he'd go and fetch birdseed from the garage with his little red tin cup and feed the birds. It always made him feel much better.

The war is over

I'm sitting in the schoolroom doing my homework, but I don't know where Anna is. She's already finished hers long ago. Asta is standing at the front door, barking. At first I think it's because of the Holumbe - it's been doing strange things in the garden lately - but the barking continues, so I go outside. It's Mr Ben, the postmaster, pushing his bicycle up the hill, sweating terribly in his khaki uniform. He waves at me but carries on around the house to the back veranda. I wonder why Mr Ben is here, because only yesterday Thambulo and I went to Maharaj's to fetch the post and Mr Ben doesn't like to leave his counter. He usually sends his assistant when there is something urgent.

I run through the house and call Mutti. When we get to the back veranda, Mr Ben is already there wiping his thick face with his handkerchief, completely out of breath.

"Aah," Mutti greets him.

"Madam, the war is over!" Mr Ben blurts out.

Mutti looks at him and then she calls VhoSarah and Mukegulu. She tells me to go and make Mr Ben some lemonade. When I come outside again, she has already gathered Anna and Willie into her arms.

"The war is over!" She is crying now, and laughing.

I give Mr Ben the lemonade.

"Isn't that wonderful, Hannes?" Mutti looks at me. "Now your father can come home again."

"Yes," I smile weakly.

"Where are Sarah and Wilhelmina?" she says, but then we see them come running up the path from the vegetable garden.

"The war is over!" Mutti shouts.

Mukegulu and VhoSarah are very happy. They hug Mutti and us and dance around her with their arms in the air, ululating.

Mutti stops and says, "What do you think I should do, Mr Ben? I mean, when do you think the Mufunzi will be released from the camp?"

"I don't know, Madam. Probably soon." He gives me the empty cup and hauls his heavy body back onto the bicycle. "I have to get back to the Post Office now. I just wanted to tell you the good news myself."

"Thank you so much Mr Ben," Mutti says, wiping her tears.

Once Mr Ben has vanished down the hill again, Mutti takes a deep breath and says shakily, "Sarah, why don't you go and make us some Berliner Pfannekuchen for coffee so we can celebrate!"

"Please can VhoSarah and Mukegulu have Pfannekuchen with us?" begs Anna.

"Of course."

Anna and I set the table for all of us and make cinnamon sugar and open a jar of mango preserve, while Mutti brews a strong pot of coffee and opens a tin of condensed milk.

"A feast fit for kings," she announces when we all sit down around the kitchen table.

"When is Father coming?" Willie wants to know.

"We have to be patient, Willie. I'm going to drive to Sibasa just now to fetch Miss Talbot. She'll know how to find things out."

Somehow we manage to close our eyes to wait for Mutti to say grace, but she can't speak properly and Mukegulu and VhoSarah start up a jubilant Easter hymn, even though Easter is over already.

"For He has risen. Hallelujah, Hallelujah!" we sing, and VhoSarah gets up to fetch the rhythm cushion. But in the middle of the song we hear a noise in the pantry - bottles falling and breaking. I jump up to go and see. A monkey has got in. Someone must have forgotten to close the doors properly. Anna helps me chase it out.

Mutti only comes back from Miss Talbot the next day. She says Miss Talbot persuaded her that it would be much better to go to the police station in Louis Trichardt in the morning, but the policemen sent them right back to the military camp near Sibasa. The military police told them that no one can know for sure when Father will be released. It could take weeks or months or even years, because first the Allies have to decide what will happen to prisoners of war, says Mrs Talbot

The first few weeks Mutti constantly nags Anna and me not to go too far away from the house just in case Father comes back. Miss Talbot tries to explain to her that she shouldn't worry so much because it will probably still take a while. But Mutti won't have any of it.

VhoSarah and Mukegulu have set about spring-cleaning the house from top to bottom. Luckily the congregation decided to whitewash the church earlier this year and Teacher Lalumbe is setting aside a period every afternoon so that the children can get the school gardens into good shape.

Mutti spends much of her time in Father's study. When she isn't making sure that the reports are all filed correctly and the accounts are up to date, she washes the curtains, dusts the books and files and wipes the pictures on the wall.

At some stage there is a rumour that all German prisoners of war are going to be deported straight back to Germany, but then we hear of men who have been released and have been allowed to go home.

Mutti's ears constantly strain for the sound of a car. She asks the truck driver who delivers Maharaj's goods to let her know immediately if he sees any military police vehicle.

And now it's already late September and Father still hasn't come home. Letters from the camp are getting scarce and it sounds as if Father himself is getting very frustrated.

VhoSarah has lit a fire in the schoolroom and we're all sitting in there, even though it is Saturday. Anna and Willie have thrown a blanket over the coffee table in the corner by the sofa and are playing under it. I can't see them but Anna seems to be putting on a puppet show because she is making different voices - a deep father voice, a kind mother voice, a shaky granny voice and a squeaky baby voice that makes Willie laugh all the time.

Mutti is sewing.

I'm working on my carving for Father for when he comes back. I'm trying to carve the scene where the prodigal son comes back home and they slaughter a calf for him. But it isn't so easy. Thambulo helped me to make the design but at the moment he's going to catechism classes and he's always busy learning.

The grandfather clock ticks loudly through all the other sounds and it seems as if I'm the only one who hears the car coming up the hill. I go to look out the window. It has begun to drizzle.

Now Mutti hears it too. She jumps up and goes outside. It's a big black car. For a moment she stands on the veranda next to Djambo and then she runs down the stairs without her raincoat on. First the driver gets out. He's smoking a cigarette. And then Father. He's wearing a white short-sleeved shirt and khaki shorts and boots. He looks darker and shorter than when I had seen him through the fence at Andalusia. His curly ginger hair is cut short and neat.

Mutti runs up to him and embraces him. Father looks embarrassed and Mutti lets him go. He goes to the back of the car and lifts out a wooden trunk and then he shakes the driver's hand.

"Anna, Anna," I whisper loudly, "Father is here." Anna and Willie don't seem to hear.

As soon as the driver is gone Father hugs Mutti. Then he looks at her and wipes a strand of hair out of her face. Mutti tightens her jersey and tries to pull Father up the stairs, but Father bends down and picks up his trunk. It seems heavy.

My heart is pounding. "Anna, Anna," I say again. "Father is here."

The door opens and Willie quickly crawls out from under the blanket and comes to stand next to me.

"I already wrote to you that we've converted the front room into a school room," Mutti says half apologetically.

Father looks around blankly. Then he sees Willie and me and his face breaks into a smile. He strides towards us.

"And who do we have here?" He pats my head awkwardly and I shake his hand firmly like Mutti has taught me. Mutti motions me to stand up straight.

"Let me look at you," he says, turning me around. "My, but you are growing into a tall boy, Johannes, in a few years you are going to overtake me."

I can feel pride spreading through my body.

Father bends down towards Willie who quickly hides behind me.

"Don't you remember me, Willie?" says Father. "You came to visit me in Andalusia, where all the soldiers were?"

Willie recoils from Father's outstretched hand.

"You must be tired, Wilhelm," says Mutti. "After such a long trip."

"Yes, I am rather." Even his voice sounds different from how I remembered it. Louder. Harsher.

"After all that waiting it happened so fast, we didn't even have time to say goodbye to each other properly. And then the three days on the train and the five-hour trip by car. Yes, I am rather tired."

Father nods towards me. "Maybe Hannes can read something for me later," he says. "After I have washed and changed into some fresh clothes."

He picks up the trunk and then he is out of the room again.

I take a deep breath.

"I don't want a strange uncle here," whines Willie.

"Go tell VhoWilhelmina and VhoSarah that the Vhafunzi has arrived," Mutti says to me before following Father down the passage.

Anna giggles from under the table. "He smells funny," she says as she crawls out. "He's forgotten me."

Then Willie, Anna, Asta and I all run off to go and tell Mukegulu and VhoSarah the good news. When we get to the mudi, VhoSarah insists on first putting on a fresh headscarf and apron. Mukegulu scolds her for taking so long and we walk back up the hill through the gentle rain to the house.

When we get back Father is standing in the kitchen with Mutti, looking dazed. He has already washed and shaved and is wearing clothes from his cupboard. They hang loosely on him. When he sees Anna he shakes her hand and gently tugs at her plaits.

"You're looking more and more like your mother every day, Anna."

Anna looks embarrassed.

"But I see you let the children out into the sun far too much, look how dark their skins have become."

VhoSarah and Mukegulu khota before Father. He is very happy to see them, but at first it seems as if he's forgotten what to do. And then he remembers.

"Ndaa!" he says, holding his hands together.

"Aah!" they reply.

There is an awkward silence and then Mukegulu and VhoSarah get up again and Mukegulu shakes her head. "I can see that they didn't give the Mufunzi enough food in the prison."

Father laughs. "My wife says you have looked after the family very well."

Mukegulu beams but VhoSarah looks very shy. Mutti asks them to prepare food for Father.

"Don't make too much," he says. "I'm not used to eating so much anymore."

"Don't worry, Vhafunzi," Mukegulu reassures him. "We'll get you fat soon again."

Mutti calls me and Anna into the schoolroom to help tidy up and move the desks so that there is more space for the sofa and the chairs again. Then we sit down and wait for Father. Mutti says we must sit up straight, and after a while he comes and sits down with us. Nobody says anything. We look at Father expectantly. Mutti clears her throat but Father doesn't notice.

"Tell us a bit about the camp, Wilhelm," Mutti starts.

Father looks at her blankly.

"Wilhelm?"

He doesn't say anything.

"You must be very tired," Mutti says. She's put on her new blue dress with the big collar. "Let's at least thank God for delivering you safely back to us all."

We close our eyes and wait for Father to start, but nothing happens. So Mutti prays.

"I think, after we've eaten, I want to go for a walk," says Father. "I haven't walked in our forest for such a long time."

15.

The red of her tail lights vanished into the dust like evil eyes. So much dust from one car, blackening and bleeding the sky. It wasn't safe to drive off at this time of day even if she had a big car. She should have waited till morning, but she was always in such a hurry. Never listened to anyone.

He had to get inside, the dust was making it hard to breathe. Gusts of wind were stirring up debris and bats. He'd never seen bats before here at Stillefontein - there were many in Venda - but never here. Maybe they were birds. He would go inside and see if he could find the binoculars. But he probably would never be able to find anything again in his house the way she had left it all upside down.

The veranda stairs seemed steeper and halfway up he had to rest a bit, catch his breath. As soon as he got to the top he sat down heavily in his chair, the floorboards creaking beneath him. He'd dreamt once, long ago, that he had fallen through into the cellar and the snakes were crawling blindly over each other, looking for a way out.

There was no one on the path this evening, only the bats in the dirty sky, blown like litter - like the end of the world. It was hard to breathe in this heat. The sweat was pouring down his neck and his shirt was chafing him. After Susanna had stormed off this morning, he'd gone and tidied up the kitchen, hoping that maybe she would come back and all would be well. They could talk more and he could explain about Kate and why he didn't want to live in Pretoria because of Anna and all the memories.

Then she had come back from her drive even angrier. Maybe it was because he had gone and fished the bags she had thrown away out of the rubbish bin and brought them back up into the kitchen. He was going to explain to her that it was good of her to clean the house, but she couldn't just throw his things away. He needed the yoghurt containers, they always came in handy. And he needed the green fly swat all the time. And the poison for the ants - they would take over the house in no time if he didn't use it.

The smell of dust and blood was making him nauseous. There was debris from the wind clattering on the tin roof. He would have to go inside. The house smelled of paraffin and poison. The flies had been bad this afternoon - maybe he'd sprayed too much Doom.

As he locked the front security gate, Johannes thought he could see lightning behind the koppies. Maybe tonight the rains would come and he would feel better. He pushed open the door to the front room. She had stripped the bed and Father's kist was sticking out from underneath. He was feeling so tired. Maybe if he ate something he would feel better. Couldn't remember if he had eaten today. He would just lie down a bit before he tidied up.

The wind was rattling at the windows, but it was soft and cool and calm in here. Maybe Susanna would come back and they could light the lamps again and sing and dance. They could even burn things if she wanted to - Father's things. His things. Anything. Yes, take them to the riverbed and make a big fire where that woman sits at night. Maybe that would bring the rain. But now he needed to lie down a bit. He was feeling so strange. Just lie here and watch the soft rose curtains darken.

When Johannes looked down at his body again, he saw that he had lost his legs. He tried to get up but he couldn't. His body was too heavy. Why had she moved the mattress onto the floor? He tried to call for help but there was no one in the house, just the wind rattling the roof.

And then the door opens. It is Thambulo.

"Look!" Johannes pleads. "My legs are gone."

Thambulo smiles. He looks so strong and handsome. Johannes wants to ask him how he has been all these years, but he can't speak. Thambulo stands there smiling, warm and kind and sad, always a bit sad. He tries to ask Thambulo to go and find his legs, he needs them. Thambulo's eyes are tender, he smiles and turns around and goes into the kitchen. Johannes looks down at his body again. Maybe Thambulo is going to bring him back his legs. Then he sees a thin black snake slither out from under the mattress, a king snake with a little crown on its head. And then the queen snake, just like in the fairy tale. More snakes crawling out of the mattress. Some black and others translucent. They are beautiful. Why had he never noticed before that they were living inside his mattress? Suddenly Father rides into the room on his horse. There is smoke coming out of its nostrils.

"Careful," he wants to shout, "you're going to trample on them."

Father looks at him but doesn't seem to see him. He is patting Bismarck on his sleek black neck, feeding him sago pudding with a long spoon. Then he gets back onto the horse and rides right through the wall leaving dust and debris. Johannes wants to follow him but he remembers that he doesn't have any legs. Thambulo comes back into the bedroom again, beckoning his friends to join him. He wants to tell Thambulo about the snakes but Thambulo too is looking past him towards the door. They are carrying a stretcher with Mukegulu on it. She is dead.

Thambulo looks at him accusingly. He wants to tell Thambulo that he is innocent. He wants to tell him that he can keep his legs to make appeasement, but Thambulo doesn't look at him. His heart hurts so, like there's a burning coal inside his chest.

The men walk through the room with the stretcher, stepping over his mattress - a sombre procession stepping through the hole in the wall that Father and Bismarck left.

And then he woke up. There was a red glow coming through the curtains. Something was burning. He could see her now through the window; the fire she made was higher than the house. He had meant to tell her so many times not to make such a big fire. Especially not in a storm. It was too dangerous.

He could see her. The prophet woman was throwing her clothes into the flames, singing, dancing around the fire – moving in closer and closer. Then she caught alight. He could see it clearly - she was burning. He had to go out and give her water. Why did he never offer her any water?

Johannes tried to lift himself off the bed but he couldn't move. He had to get hold of Jooste. Her flesh was burning. Her hair. There was no smell, just fire. The rainmaker was dancing wildly, sparks and ashes whirling about her ghostly figure. He looked away. He had to concentrate on moving, getting up. Finally he managed to will his heavy legs over the side of the bed and crawled towards the front door. It was locked. So many locks. He had to get to the kitchen. Fetch the keys so he could try to save her. Put out the fire and let her into his house.

Father holds his first service

A few days after he's come back from Andalusia, Father conducts his first Sunday service. We all walk to the church together - Father and Mutti in front, and Anna, Willie and me behind. Asta follows us. It's a beautiful spring day, with the dark red boerhuilboom trees in full blossom and the white frothy mayflower and pink prunus lining the path to the church. Father says that after living in a semi-desert for all these years his eyes have to get used to all this abundance. He says he'd forgotten how lush and fertile Wittenberg really is.

Today there is no need to ring the church bell for a second time. The congregation already lines the path. As soon as they see us they break into song - men, women and children, all dressed in their best clothes, holding out branches of blossoms, smiling at the Vhafunzi who has returned to them. There is clapping and dancing and ululation. Many heathens dressed in their colourful salempores have also come to welcome back the Vhafunzi. Father looks very grand in his black Luther robe. He smiles, greets and shakes everyone's hands.

At the door of the church Evangelist David and some of the church elders in black suits greet us. As soon as we enter, the singing changes to a slower Lutheran hymn about entering the House of God and we walk through the church towards the altar in a slow swaying procession.

Anna waves at Noria who is standing with her father and mother. Thambulo isn't here because Mukegulu has sent him home to Nshelele to attend the first initiation school. She hasn't told Mutti or Father.

When we have all settled onto the benches, Evangelist David opens the service with a prayer. He thanks God for bringing back safely His shepherd so that He may lead the mighty flock and prevent them from straying. The lead singer gets up and starts another hymn, beating his rhythm cushion. The congregation joins in and the sun pours over us through the red and blue windows. Today it feels - as Mutti likes to say - as if our little church is truly swelling with God's great harmony.

Finally Father climbs up onto the high pulpit.

"In the name of the Father, the Son and the Holy Ghost," he booms.

The congregation murmurs with excitement. And then he starts his sermon. He tells us about his time in Andalusia and how, even in the midst of the most difficult circumstances, God still pours out His blessings. He tells us how his time there gave him the opportunity to be with many other Vhafunzi. How, while sitting behind barbed wire fences, the men spoke endlessly about their work in their congregations across South Africa.

"And always we found guidance from this book," Father holds up the Bible. "Each one of us held our own congregations in our heart and mind and so often we ended our discussions with a prayer for you all."

For a moment I think Father is going to cry but then he goes on to talk about the Great War in Europe that has just ended and how Satan has used the opportunity to turn people against each other.

"One thing I have learnt is that Satan loves war," Father speaks forcefully. "Because it gives him the opportunity to bring hatred and confusion into our lives. The chaos of war is like food to Satan. Satan loves chaos!" Father's Tshivenda is still perfect.

"But chaos, my dear congregation, is not just something you find in times of war. No, Satan also loves peaceful times - when everybody is just carrying on with their lives and becomes complacent about their faith." Father pauses dramatically. "Just think how nice and peacefully Adam and Eve were living in the Garden of Eden. They had everything. The place was full of mangoes and pawpaws and litchis and avocados and bananas growing on the trees. There was also plenty of bushmeat. Just like here in Venda." There is tittering among the congregation.

"And it was exactly because Adam and Eve were not looking where they were going - because they were becoming complacent - that they did not notice the Serpent slithering down from the tree and into the grass, ready to tempt them."

"Amen," shouts one of the heathen women. Father looks startled, but he continues.

"It is exactly when we think that everything is going well that Satan will come up to us and tempt us."

"Amen," the woman says again. Anna nudges me and I try not to giggle. Mutti looks at us admonishingly.

"Like when we are visiting nicely among our heathen relatives and the Serpent whispers to us: 'Go ahead, slaughtering a goat for the ancestors isn't against Christianity. Oh, and how can going out in the night to pick a bit of mushanga be wrong? It's our culture after all."

There is laughter in the church. I think Father's a very good preacher. Mutti always told us that he was much better than Uncle Els.

"But, my dear congregation," he continues, "the danger lies not in slaughtering something for the ancestors or in taking a bit of mushanga for a cough or for a bad stomach. No, the danger lies in being complacent and in sliding back into our old heathen ways just because it is easier if we don't always have to argue with our relatives." Father pauses. "It also means we can get as drunk as we like at the next dhava work party and then come back to this church and ask for forgiveness the next Sunday!"

The congregation laughs and some of the heathen women start to talk to each other. The Evangelists get up and tell them to keep quiet.

"No, my dear brothers and sisters in Christ," Father continues. "What we have to remember is that Satan is like a snake on a hot summer's day - just as you are about to start cooking he will surprise you by sliding out of the ashes from under your cooking pot. Or he may lie lazily on the path to the river when you go and fetch water, pretending to be a stick. At night he will come and look for warmth in your bed or find the roosting place of your chickens and kill them. Because Satan knows when we are relaxing in the Garden of Eden."

Anna nudges me again but this time I ignore her.

"No, my dear congregation, we have to keep our eyes open at all times."

The congregation is quiet now. I watch the dust dance in the sunbeam near the altar and start to feel a bit dozy.

Finally Father closes his eyes and starts to pray.

As he climbs down the steps of the pulpit the congregation once more bursts into jubilant song. Mutti takes his hand and squeezes it as soon as Father sits down next to her. Father wipes the sweat off his forehead with his white handkerchief. He turns towards me and smiles. His face is glowing. I smile back.

Lots of people come to Holy Communion, but first there is general confession, so the service is extra long today. Finally, after the collection, we all go out into the sunshine. Everyone is keen to shake the hands of their Mufunzi and Father tells them how happy he is to be back.

In the week many members of the congregation have brought gifts of chickens, vegetables and fruit to our house to welcome back the Mufunzi. Before church Mukegulu and VhoSarah have used some of the food to prepare a special Sunday lunch for us. There is roast chicken with applesauce and fried potatoes and pumpkin fritters and cooked green beans. For pudding we are going to have preserved mangoes with vanilla cream. Mutti says that these are all Father's favourite foods.

Anna, Willie and I quickly help her to finish setting the table. Today we are not eating in the kitchen but at the big dining room table in the schoolroom and Mutti has put out her best white tablecloth and the dinner service with the little green patterns she got as a wedding gift. Mutti even sets a wineglass for her and Father. We get lemonade.

We have to wait a while before we can eat because Father is getting changed out of his suit and is putting away his notes. When he finally walks into the room, he looks happy and relaxed.

"How good it is to be back again," he beams. "I was thinking just now that the only way I'm going to get this wonderful mission station back on track is by drawing up a three-month plan." Father sits down at the head of the table. "Because if there's one thing I've learnt from life in the camp, it's that if you don't bring order and discipline into your life immediately, you might as well give up."

"Wasn't your father's sermon inspiring today?" Mutti says.

We nod our heads.

"I tell you Elisabeth, we would have all gone mad in Andalusia if we hadn't been so disciplined."

Mutti points at the chicken and he picks up the carving knife and fork and stands up. We watch him as he poises himself over the bird. "By Christmas you won't recognise this place. The first part of my plan is to draw up a new register of all the people staying at Wittenberg. Then I'm going to make a roster of the amount of days a month each family has to work on the church lands. Evangelist David tells me that our Christians have become too lazy to give of their labour."

Father uses the carving fork to explain. He hasn't been talking this much since he came back from Andalusia. Anna is starting to fidget.

"I'll have to go and negotiate for more land with Chief Ravhura. We'll probably have to demarcate new pieces of land to the families that have grown. Clear some forest."

Mutti nods encouragingly and finally Father begins to carve the chicken, slicing away at the white breast meat which none of us like. "This knife is blunt," he announces and I quickly jump up to go and fetch the sharpener from the kitchen.

"You know Elisabeth, I know I've said this before, but I keep realising how much of a gift my time in Andalusia really was." Father sharpens the knife. "It's given me time to reflect on the purpose of our work here in Africa."

Father starts to dish out pieces of chicken but then he stops again in mid-air. "And the sense of fellowship and collegiality amongst the missionaries and pastors, you can't even begin to imagine how strong and enriching that was."

At last we each receive our share of the chicken and Mutti dishes up the potatoes.

"It must have been wonderful, Wilhelm." Mutti indicates to us children that we should help ourselves to the vegetables. I help Willie.

"Next month I also want to start christening all the Christian children that were born while I was away. And then we can start to christen heathens again." Father is getting excited now. "I know Missionary Els did christenings but Evangelist David tells me that there is still a big backlog."

Finally Father says grace and Mutti raises her glass to him.

"I know you have been very busy." Father eats fast. "But Elisabeth, I noticed that our front garden is looking terrible."

Anna and I try not to look at each other.

"It looks just like an nganga's yard. What are all those piles of stones and the bones and skulls of animals?"

"For some reason or other Samuel refuses to clean the front garden," Mutti says. "He says there's a cobra living among the rocks."

Father shakes his head. "No matter how long they are exposed to Christianity, the vhaVenda will always be superstitious." He wipes his mouth with the serviette. "The food is delicious. It's been four years since I have eaten the pope's nose!" He laughs. Then he carries on. "But if there's a snake why didn't you ask Missionary Els to shoot it?"

"I couldn't ask Rolf to do everything." Mutti looks upset. "He lives far."

There's silence around the table. Father looks at our plates and helps himself to more chicken and potatoes. After a while he says, "Forgive me Elisabeth. I have to keep reminding myself how difficult these years must have been for you."

Mutti gets up and clears the plates.

Father turns towards me and Anna. "And the two of you? Are you ready for proper school in Pretoria next year?"

I nod my head.

"Miss Talbot's been reading poetry to us," Anna tells Father. "Do you know Wilfred Owen? He was a soldier in the Great War."

Father hasn't heard of him.

"His name is not spelt the same as Uncle Els' Wilfried."

"Are you friends with the Els boys?" Father asks.

Anna and I shrug our shoulders and Mutti comes back into the dining room with the pudding. She looks as if she's been crying.

"I'm sure your mother has been the best teacher." Father takes Mutti's hand and smiles at her. "Maybe before they go off to big school I can give the children catechism classes and German grammar lessons? What do you think?"

Mutti dishes up the pudding and passes around the ice cream.

"But I think we'll need to move the school into the storeroom next to my office, which I have noticed is being used as a chicken coop."

Mutti pushes away her pudding, uneaten. "I told you why we moved the chicken coop there, Wilhelm. We were losing all our eggs and I didn't know what to do anymore."

"Forgive me dearest." Father takes Mutti's hand again. "I know I'm being a bit impossible. I'm just not used to you all anymore."

Mutti sighs and starts to eat her pudding.

"I'll go and fix the chicken coop tomorrow," he says. "Then I can patrol it for a few nights to make sure that nothing steals our eggs."

I want to explain to Father that it is Asta who is stealing eggs and that she is too old now to learn and that we have to leave her alone.

Father must be very hungry because he is dishing himself another plate of pudding. "What do you say Elisabeth, after lunch we all lie down for a bit?"

He winks at Mutti.

16.

Someone was singing on the veranda. It was a child's voice. Johannes opened his eyes. How strange. He was lying on Susanna's bed in the middle of the day. The room looked so clean and tidy; the light was streaming through the half-opened curtains. There were flowers next to the bed - roses. He tried to lift himself up but couldn't. His body was too heavy.

The singing stopped. The child was rocking on his chair, talking to herself. He had to warn her not to rock too hard, the floorboards were getting thin and she could fall through into the cellar. He tried again to lift himself but his body refused. All he seemed to be able to do was pick up his hand but that too kept falling down again, causing the shimmering dust to dance around him. He could feel the tears trickling down his face, gathering warmly in his neck. He tried to wipe them away but couldn't.

It was dark when he woke up again. Someone was coming down the passage towards the room. It was a woman. She was talking to the child. It wasn't VhoSarah. This woman was speaking in Sesotho. He could smell onions and meat frying in the kitchen and the radio was playing hymns. They must have gone to town to buy batteries.

The door opened and the woman came into the room. She was dressed in a blue skirt and white T-shirt. It was Grace. How did she get into the house? He must have forgotten to lock the front door. Johannes followed her solid form with his eyes as she closed the flowery curtains and switched on the lamp next to the bed. The light was pink and soft. Kate had bought the lamp for Susanna's room. She'd been afraid of the dark as a child, wanted a light burning next to her bed all night long.

"Batho, Mr Weber! You are awake!" Grace sat down next to him, taking his hands into hers. He closed his eyes for a moment to absorb her touch. The tears again, he couldn't stop them. She wiped his face gently. She looked older from up close. He could see grey hair sticking out from under the maroon beret. Her eyes were soft with age. Like Mukegulu's.

"I must tell Susanna that you are awake." She stood up and walked towards the door. He wanted to ask her to stay a little longer but no words came out of his mouth.

Grace came back soon, holding a cell phone. "She will be so excited."

Pulane had followed her from the kitchen and she looked at him from the passage, wide-eyed. He lifted his hand to beckon her in.

"I'm not sure when he woke up," Grace spoke into the phone. "I walked in just now and his eyes were open."

There was a pause.

"He doesn't seem to be able to say much, but that's what we're told to expect."

Another pause.

"Don't worry. He's fine, he's fine."

The little girl was staring at him. He tried to smile at her.

"No, he hasn't said anything yet. He's just woken up now. I'll call the specialist in the morning."

Grace put the phone in her pocket and sat down next to him again.

"Susanna sends her love." She motioned to Pulane to come inside. "Come and say hullo to Mr Weber." But the little girl withdrew further into the passage.

"She's a bit scared of you," Grace laughed. "It's probably all those pipes."

For the first time he noticed the urine bag and drip hanging from a stand next to his bed.

Grace shook her head. "You gave us all such a fright. If Susanna hadn't asked me to come and clean, you'd probably be dead."

He wanted to tell her that his bladder was full.

"When I got here I called and called and then I saw that the lights inside your house were all still on, so I went to fetch Mr Jooste. He brought his sons and they broke the lock on the gate and the front door. They had to use an angle grinder to get inside."

Johannes squeezed her hand.

Grace squeezed back. "You had a stroke, Mr Weber," she said. "On the right side. You might struggle to speak."

He couldn't hold it in any longer so he let go of his bladder. It was hard to know if it was shame or relief that was spreading through his body.

"And now I'm going to give you a nice wash and a massage." He held onto her hand tightly, he didn't want her to go.

"I'm not going to leave you, Mr Weber. We're staying right here in your house, me and Pulane, until you are better." Johannes was relieved.

"I hope you don't mind, but Susanna felt it was better to put you into this room. It's much brighter and cooler in here," she said. "Pulane and I are staying in your bedroom."

The **Mission Trip**

Father can't stop talking about his three-month plan. "By Christmas you won't recognise this place," he keeps telling everyone.

The first thing he does is to buy a riding horse from a German farmer near Louis Trichardt. Its name is Blackie. Father says it's much easier to inspect the mission farm on horseback and, besides, he isn't so good at driving the Ford yet. He's getting driving lessons from Dr Talbot and Missionary Els, but they don't always have time. Mutti says she could teach him but Father laughs and says it's probably better if husbands don't learn driving from their wives.

All day Father is out on his horse filling in the registers and making a list of people who need to be christened or confirmed. Sometimes on weekends he takes me with him because he says it isn't good for a boy to spend so much time in his room. He takes me on Blackie and I sit in front. He says that when he has time he is going to teach me how to ride.

We ride from mudi to mudi and Father asks people a whole lot of questions, making notes in his black book. He gets angry if they haven't put whitewashed stones on the edges of their demarcated lands. Sometimes he checks if they have taken more land than they were supposed to. When that happens, he scolds them and makes them move the white stones to the correct position. Then they complain and say that their families have grown since the Mufunzi first measured the land, but Father says that they can't just take the land. It has to be done according to protocol.

Father has already gone to visit Chief Ravhura to pay his respects. He tells me that he has also discussed getting more land for the Mission. Father says Chief Ravhura is a fine man.

He also says that maybe one day I can go to agricultural college and then I can take over the running of the Mission farm so that he can concentrate on his real work, which is spreading the word of God.

Yesterday after school, Father called me into his office and asked if I wanted to go on a mission trip with him in the Ford.

"It will be good for my driving skills if I do a longer journey in the car by myself."

I'm excited because we're going to visit Chief Tshivhase. Everybody knows that he gives the Evangelists a lot of trouble.

We leave early in the morning when it is still dark because it's a long trip. Father drives well, just sometimes he drives a bit fast and I worry that he won't be able to brake quickly enough. Our first stop is at Tshakuma River where we drink the coffee with condensed milk and sandwiches that Mutti made for us.

As we approach Chief Tshivhase's mudi, we overtake a group of young women walking up the hill in single file, carrying drums and bundles of clothes on their heads. They must be going to domba. They laugh and wave at us.

"At least our heathens don't walk around half naked like the people around here." Father waves back at them.

We park outside the chief's courtyard and Father puts on his long black morning jacket and gives me his comb for my hair. A short, bald man comes to the car. We greet him and Father tells him why we have come. The man takes us to a large cooking hut. Soon three women arrive, carrying food and a calabash full of water. Before they reach us they kneel down and walk towards us on their knees. I hope it does not hurt them. When they get to us they lie down on the ground at our feet.

"Get up, women," Father says. "You don't need to lie down before a Christian. We bend our knees to only one king, and that is God the Creator."

One of the women pours water into a bowl so that we can wash our hands. Then they leave again on their knees. Father says that we have to eat something otherwise we will be seen to be insulting the chief. He says that once he even had to eat monkey meat at a chief's kraal so as not to insult him.

Somewhere the drumming starts. I wish I could go and watch them dance. Noria has told me the Tshivase are very good dancers.

After a while the short man returns and leads us to the chief's courtyard. Chief Tshivhase is a big strong man with a long beard. He's wearing a hat with a wide brim and a hunting jacket, and there's a rifle slung over his shoulder. Father told me in the car that the chief likes to dress like the old Boer generals.

We khota and exchange greetings.

"I see that the Mufunzi has taught his son manners."

"I came to show my son how much love the Chief has for Mudzimo," Father replies.

The chief looks at me and smiles through his beard. His teeth are very white. "Well then, we will have to give the young man a present to show how much we respect your god."

The drumming is getting louder. It's domba. Chief Tshivhase nods at the man who brought us to him and he whispers something to another man who quickly leaves. Chief Tshivhase points at two straight-backed chairs and we sit down.

"I see that the girls are gathering for the domba," Father says, starting up the conversation again. "When does it begin?"

"Yes, we have many girls this year." Chief Tshivhase looks at me. "Do you know the meaning of the domba, young man?"

I can feel my face getting red and look away.

Father shifts in his chair. He clears his throat and says, "Chief Tshivhase, let me get to the point. I have come to ask you why you are obstructing our work among your people."

"Not so fast, Vhafunzi. First I want to know why your great nation lost the war."

Father looks him straight in the eyes. "As a man of God I am not so much interested in worldly battles, I am more interested in the battles of the spirit."

There is a commotion at one of the entrances of the courtyard as five young bulls are lead in by a group of men.

Father ignores them. "It is no use resisting Mudzimo, Chief Tshivhase. Even your father knew that He is more powerful than any chief on earth."

Chief Tshivhase looks at the beasts for a few moments. Slowly he takes his gun off his shoulder and points it, like a stick, at a young red bull with white spots on its back. The men hold onto its horns and push down its head. The man who received us picks up a spear, steps towards it and stabs it in the back of its neck. It falls down immediately. Someone cuts open its throat while another man catches the blood in a bowl.

Father seems to be ignoring the slaughter of the young bull in front of us. "He will find your soul Chief, and bring light to it. Even if you try to hide in your tradition."

"How many times do I have to tell you and your people, Vhafunzi, that my soul is not in darkness," the chief laughs. "I am a leader and I will not tell my people to change what they have been doing for many, many years, just because you say so."

The men start to hack the young beast into pieces with an axe. I notice the chief looking at me and immediately sit up in my chair. The air smells of smoke, salt and blood. I can hear the girls singing a song that Thambulo taught Anna and me and Noria long ago.

"You see, Vhafunzi," the chief continues. "It is your education that gives you power, not your God. Your God makes our people weak. I have seen that."

Father points at the sky. "I mean you no disrespect Chief Tshivhase, but could it be that you are confusing power in this world with the true power of the spirit?"

The chief nods at the men and one of them comes forward with the hindquarter of the young bull and lays it down in front of me. I bring my hands together in thanks. Some women arrive with large enamel dishes and gather the chunks of meat.

Father and the chief talk and argue for a long time. I try to listen to the singing and watch some children playing outside the courtyard. I wish Thambulo was here, maybe we could have gone to watch the girls dancing. My eyes keep getting drawn to the hindquarter, which is attracting a host of flies. Chief Tshivhase must have noticed this because suddenly he interrupts the conversation.

"Rather than worrying about my soul, Vhafunzi, shouldn't you be teaching your son not to be afraid of blood?"

"I'm not afraid," I mumble.

When we finally get into the car, Father is in a bad mood. Then the Ford doesn't want to start and Father says he shouldn't have parked it uphill because then the petrol can't get through. At last it starts and we drive off down the narrow track. The hindquarter, which didn't fit into the boot, is lying on the back seat. We pass a group of girls and women on their way to the domba. This time Father doesn't wave at them.

"Sometimes I think we are wasting our time here in Venda. These people are far too arrogant to hear the Word."

To keep the flies out of the car, we have to keep all the windows closed and it's very hot. Father drives very fast and I hold onto the door tightly. The smell of the hindquarter is getting stronger. My stomach feels funny and then I'm sick. Father swerves off the road, just missing a tree and we come to a stop.

"I'm so sorry," I say. "I didn't know."

Father sighs and I get out of the car and am sick again into the tall grass. Father takes off his jacket and tries to clean up the mess on the seat with a greasy rag. I try to help him but it just makes me sick again.

Father hands me his handkerchief and we get back into the car and carry on until we get to the next river.

"My Brothers in Germany can't even begin to understand the conditions we have to work under here in Africa," Father mumbles as he stops.

I wash my face and hands in the river. I wish I could take off my clothes and swim, but Father collects water in the canteen and is washing out the rag and rubbing away at the stain on the seat. The rest of the way to Wittenberg we drive in silence.

When we get home it's late afternoon already. I quickly go to my room to take off my Sunday clothes. Mutti calls me to go and fetch Anna and Willie from outside.

They are playing in the Holumbe's garden. I don't know what they are playing but Anna has lit a candle and put it inside Djambo's skull and everything looks a bit spooky in the dusk.

"Did you ask Mutti if you can take a candle?" I ask.

A monkey is sitting in the lower branches of the Stinkwood.

"What are you doing?" I ask. The monkey is picking ants off the branch and eating them.

"What's the matter, Anna?" Anna and Willie look upset.

"Did you know that Germany lost the War?" Anna finally says. "Why did Father never tell us? Or Mutti?"

"I don't know." The candle flickers. The monkey chatters in the tree. "Mutti says that you and Willie must come inside now. It's getting late."

"What if the English attack us here at Wittenberg?" Anna says.

"They won't."

"I dreamt that they killed Father."

"You won't believe what Chief Tshivhase gave me today."

Anna ignores me.

"The Holumbe doesn't want to listen." Willie points at the monkey in the tree. "It's been making scary noises the whole afternoon."

"That's not the Holumbe, Willie, it's a monkey," I say.

"Of course that's the Holumbe," says Anna.

The monkey looks at me and continues to pick the ants off the branch, popping them into its mouth, eating them, one by one, like sweets.

17

Where was Kate? He hadn't seen her for such a long time. Probably out in the garden with Foxy, picking roses for the house. He wished she would come inside soon, it was getting dark. He tried to call her. She could come and sit next to him, tell him about the roses and all her wonderful plans for the garden.

Finally the door opened.

"What a beautiful smile you have, Mr Weber," Grace said as she put down the washbowl with the warm water onto the chair next to his bed. Then she turned to close the door.

When she came back, she lifted the blanket and started to unbutton his pyjama shirt. Johannes flinched.

"Don't worry, Pappie." She pushed her arm behind him, lifting him expertly and gently prized off his shirt.

"Susanna came immediately. She was on her way to the sea when I called her. Shame. But she came back straight away and organised everything."

His body rested heavily against her arm. She smelt so clean - of roses and Vaseline. She dipped a facecloth into the steaming dish and started to wash him.

"That one," she shook her head, "she's such a good organiser. As soon as she got to the hospital in Welkom, she told the specialist that it would be better if I looked after you here at home. She said you were the kind of person who could die from being in a hospital. She even persuaded him to come and do house-visits. And the physio." She pulled down his trousers. Johannes moved his hand to ward her off. But it was no use, so he closed his eyes and surrendered to her touch.

Stupid tears - wouldn't stop.

"Shame, poor Susie. I could see she was so sick herself. When she left, apparently she got to Beaufort West and collapsed. They put her in hospital for three days and now she is staying on her friend's farm. Her mother is looking after her, Antie Liesbet. The doctor says she needs lots of rest."

Soft hands rubbing oil on him, deftly removing the catheter from his penis. Just not get an erection. An old man's shame. Back. Arms. Buttocks. Legs. Feet. Hands.

"I'm sure she'll be well enough to come visit soon though. She's just so happy that you have woken up."

He opened his eyes and looked at Grace.

"She took the Moruti's wooden box with her, the one that was under the bed. She said to tell you."

When Grace was done, she laid him against the pillows and combed his hair. He wanted her not to stop touching him. He wanted to smell her and listen to her voice.

As she made her way to the door to leave he could feel his body panic. He needed her to stay, he had so many questions. He needed to know about the prophet. He needed to know if they had managed to save her from the fire.

"Relax Pappie, just relax," Grace said as she came back to the bed and patted his hand. "The more you relax, the sooner you'll get better."

Johannes closed his eyes. He was very, very tired.

Sago pudding

Since our trip to Chief Tshivhase, Father's been too busy to take me with him anywhere again. In fact we don't see much of Father. Mostly in the day he rides out on Blackie, while at night he sits in his study and works. Nowadays, we children often eat our evening meals alone, while Mutti waits for Father and then they eat later. Since Father has been back we also have our prayers and singing in the morning before breakfast. The singing isn't so nice without Mukegulu and VhoSarah and we mostly sing German hymns.

I'm happy when we eat without Father because it means that Father and Anna can't fight, especially about sago pudding. It seems that Father forgets all the time that Anna doesn't like it. She hates it. Even though she has told him many times that she can't get it down her throat - that it gets stuck there - Father insists that Mutti makes sago pudding.

"When are we going to have sago pudding again?" he asks cheerfully and our hearts sink because we already know what is going to happen.

"Eat up young lady," he says as he watches Anna trying to swallow a spoon of the pudding.

"I can't," Anna says. "It doesn't want to go down."

"I only gave you a little," says Father, holding his own plate out for Mutti to dish up more for him.

But that doesn't help Anna. "It's like eating frogs' eggs, I can't eat it."

"At least finish what's on your plate."

"I can't," Anna says and her eyes start to fill with tears.

"Tears are not going to help, young lady. We often have to do things we don't want to."

So we sit and sit, waiting for Anna to finish her pudding.

"You two can go out and play," Father says finally, and Willie and I quickly run outside.

Sometimes Anna and Father sit at the table for hours. We can hear them, Anna tearful or angry and Father's stern voice admonishing her.

But catechism classes are even worse. Father has decided that before we go to school in Pretoria in January, Anna and I must at least have a few catechism classes. So on Friday afternoons we sit in our little schoolroom next to his office and learn psalms off by heart, as well as hymns, verses and long sections from Dr Martin Luther's Little Catechism. Anna tries her best, but she really can't remember easily.

"Don't fidget so," Father snaps at her. "Tell me, what is the Sacrament of the Baptism?"

Anna always mixes up everything - the Sacrament of Confession and the Sacrament of Baptism and all the sins we carry and the Old Adam who has to be drowned or confessed and then she can't help it anymore and asks questions like, "What about the people who never meet a missionary in their life, will they go to hell? Why can't God save them?"

After a while Father gets annoyed and says, "You will have to learn, young lady, that before one can ask so many questions one has to have a solid knowledge of the basics."

Then Anna struggles even more to learn anything off by heart and Father thinks she does it on purpose and accuses her of being wilful.

"I can't believe that your mother and I have produced such a stubborn daughter," he says.

Sometimes, after catechism classes, Anna and I go and sit in the old treehouse together and I try to calm her down.

"Maybe you must try to understand Father," I tell her. "He has been in the camp for a long time."

"But according to him everything was perfect in Andalusia," she says. "Sometimes I wish he would just go back."

"You mustn't say that Anna! You know that Father is trying to do the work of God among the heathens and they are stubborn and don't really listen to him. It's hard for him."

"But God doesn't care whether I eat sago pudding or not."

I've noticed that since Father has been back Anna has been playing with her doll Ella again. Today she has brought her up into the treehouse with her.

"I wish you wouldn't always be on Father's side." She combs Ella's hair with her fingers.

"I'm not."

If only Thambulo would come back soon so that we can go hunting or swimming or just walk in the forest.

And then something starts to steal the eggs again.

A shot rings through the night and I wake up. And then three more.

"Asta!" I panic. "He mustn't shoot Asta."

I want to run outside but it is too dark. Anna is breathing deeply in the bed next to me. A while later I hear Father's footsteps making their way past our bedroom. He is wearing his riding boots.

As soon as the door to their bedroom closes, I tiptoe through the dark passage, careful not to make the floorboards creak. The big clock in our old schoolroom ticks heavily. When I reach the strip of light that comes from under Mutti and Father's door, I stop and listen.

"You should have seen it rear up, Elisabeth. It was a huge one. I had to shoot it three times." The bed creaks under Father's weight.

Thank God it wasn't Asta.

"I threw it onto the compost heap, but I'm almost hundred percent sure it was a Mozambican Spitting cobra."

Suddenly I feel cold.

"I'll ask Samuel to burn it tomorrow." His boots thud onto the floor. "I'm also going to sort out those monkeys tomorrow. They have really taken over our orchard."

I can hear Father get up from the bed again.

"Half-eaten mangoes everywhere. You've seen it yourself, Elisabeth, just as the mangoes are about to get ripe they bite into them and then throw them away."

He pours water from the jug into the basin and starts washing himself. I can imagine what he must look like, standing there in his khaki pants, with strong freckled arms and red-blonde hairs on his chest sticking out from under his vest.

"I tried so many things," Mutti says. "But they're just not afraid of women at all. You must just see it." She laughs in her angry way. "If VhoSarah or I try to chase them, they look at us and continue to eat. But if Samuel goes there, they run away immediately."

"I'll definitely have to do something about that."

"And they're so clever. They always raid the garden when we're in church. They wait for the second or third bell and then they come and eat their fill."

I'm about to tiptoe back to our room when Mutti says, "Wilhelm, you mustn't be so harsh on the children. It wasn't easy for them without the guiding hand of a father."

The passage goes dark. Father must have blown out the candle. The bedsprings creak again.

"Our Anna just seems stubborn," Mutti says. "She's actually a good and helpful child."

"But she is so wilful. And that's not a good quality in a girl."

There is silence.

"I'm sorry Elisabeth," Father's voice is muffled so I move closer to the door. "I've been living among men for too long, it seems all a bit complicated to be with children and women again."

Mutti doesn't reply.

"But I'm worried about our children. They think they can just do what they want. When they grow up they're going to find it hard to live among people."

"Don't forget to check that the mosquito net is properly secured," I hear Mutti say.

18

The room was littered with Grandfather's papers. Looking out of the deep-set window of the cottage, Susanna could see Antie Liesbet busying herself in the yard. The old woman had been working so hard today, carrying wood into the kitchen, sweeping the yard like nobody's business. Earlier Susanna had seen her run after a squawking chicken, grab it firmly under her skinny brown arm and wring its neck. It made Susanna feel guilty for just sitting here all day, reading through Grandfather and Grandmother's correspondence, and some of Dad's things – letters to Auntie Anna, full of love and longing for their childhood.

When she had gone to sort out things at Stillefontein and Dad was in hospital after his stroke, she had decided to pack Grandfather's kist into the car and bring it with her here to Oorlogspoort. And now, when she was supposed to start working on her PhD, she had gotten drawn into the world of Grandfather and Grandmother Weber's life in Wittenberg. In the beginning she could barely remember enough German to understand the letters and struggled even more with the formal language of the mission reports. After trying for a few days, she had finally dragged herself away from her cottage to make the fifty kilometre trip to the Colesberg library to pick up a German dictionary.

Somehow, instead of stoking her old anger, going through the kist was calming. Maybe it was the tea that Antie Liesbet was bringing her every morning. She said it was for the heart. Antie Liesbet knew a thing or two.

"If anyone can make you right again, it's my mother," Althea had assured her.

Just every now and again, when she read how Grandfather was patronizing and mocking the people he worked amongst, her irritation flared up, but nothing like the anger in the past. Instead she noticed the tenderness and practicality with which Grandmother had tried to keep things together in Wittenberg during the war. And her little victories. In one letter to Grandfather she had written:

'I wondered how I would construct a right angle so that the people could build rectangular corners. At first I thought that I would have to saw off a door to measure a right angle and then I remembered the theory of Pythagoras and created a right angle with sticks and string on the red soil of Venda. I was so proud of myself.'

Amongst all the busyness and activities, Grandmother still noticed the colour of the soil. Shortly before she died she wrote to Dad. "And you know, dear Hannes, I did learn to love Wittenberg like no other place in the world. It was my paradise. It was there that, for the time that Wilhelm was away in Andalusia, I tasted real freedom."

While Grandfather was in the camp, he kept busy by plotting his flock's constriction, always worrying about his mission station far away, intellectualising, strategising:

"Venda is and will remain a difficult path for us with many obstacles on the way, even if sometimes it does feel that things are getting better. But the Holy Spirit blows wherever it wants to. And it might even possess the hearts of our people."

And Grandmother responds with her concern for her children who have all got whooping cough and how she had force-fed their dog Asta an egg filled with chilli powder to prevent her from stealing eggs. The time she had walked through the night with VhoSarah to pray for a woman who was dying in childbirth and how afterwards she had cried bitterly for the little baby. And the references to Dad – Little Hannes - who always tried so hard to be a good boy. Auntie Anna, dreamy and funny and wilful. And poor Uncle Willie who always seemed to be sick with something - asthma, malaria, TB.

Grandfather was such a hardworking man, almost obsessive. You could see he wanted to be a truly good missionary - keeping meticulous records, working through the night to translate hymns into Tshivenda and preparing his sermons. The camp years seemed to have intensified his resolve - all he wanted to do when he came back was to build and organise things and to protect his family and congregation from the dark and invading forces of nature.

Susanna got up and stretched her body. It was time to go to the main house and make coffee for her and Antie Liesbet, else she would get a scolding for sitting indoors too long. She put on her boots and opened the bright blue door of the cottage where she was greeted by the clear warm Karoo air. She had to hand it to Althea. When Susanna had called her from Colesberg in utter despair, she immediately organised with her mom that Susanna could go and stay with her. It wasn't quite the sea, but at least she was only a few hours' drive from Dad in case he got worse. Besides, the sky was infinitely blue and all you could see between here and the koppies was Karoo scrub and a few sheep.

The kitchen was hot. Antie Liesbet had stoked up the old Aga and was standing at the table slapping and kneading a piece of dough, ready for the breadpan. The room smelled of rosemary, butter, cinnamon and roasting chicken. Antie Liesbet's leathery skin was shining. She was obviously preparing a feast, just like Althea used to do on Sundays for the two of them.

"I was wondering when you were going to leave your room and all those papers," Antie Liesbet said.

Susanna went to fetch the coffee and condensed milk from the pantry.

"It isn't good if you stay in your room too long when the sun is out. Makes your insides go stale."

Susanna busied herself with the coffee pot on the stove and started to read the yellowing newspaper that lay on the kitchen table. When the coffee was done, she pulled out a chair for Antie Liesbet and sat down on the teabox watching the old woman deftly peel a large blue pumpkin.

Susanna poured the thick coffee into their cups. Finally Antie Liesbet wiped her hands on her apron and joined her. She sipped the coffee slowly, closing her eyes.

"I don't know how a city girl like you can make such good coffee," she said, just as she did every afternoon. It was part of their ritual. And every afternoon Susanna explained that she had bought the coffee in Colesberg and that next time she went she would bring Antie Liesbet as much of it as she liked.

"Still, it's the best coffee I have ever drunk," was the response.

"Did I ever tell you about the Fishwoman?" Antie Liesbet was always full of stories.

Susanna sat back and poured herself another cup of coffee.

"She lives at the fountain," the old woman said, pointing far into the koppies.

"She's very dangerous. If you're not strong enough she will pull you into the water." Antie Liesbet shook her head. "And that will be the last we ever see of you."

Susanna laughed, "All my life I've been wanting to get to the water, but every time I try something happens. I was on my way to the sea when Dad had his stroke." Watching Antie Liesbet cutting the pumpkin into cubes made her feel dejected. She should probably be with Dad right now. That's what Antie Liesbet would have done. Dropped everything and gone and look after him. Mom too. But she wasn't like them. She was too messed up.

"Isn't it time to phone your father again?"

The tears were welling up again. So many tears. In the beginning she had been foolish enough to think that Antie Liesbet hadn't noticed all the crying. She had told her that she had flu. And Antie Liesbet had left her alone to sleep, bringing food to her room three times a day. But one morning she had knocked on the door with a cup of cold bitter-smelling tea.

"Drink this," she had said. "It's jakkalsbos and rooivergeetwortel."

Every morning she had watched Susanna drink the tea. "It will make your heart strong again."

A week later she had told Susanna to walk to the koppies. They were far away and her limbs seemed so heavy, but somehow Susanna had dragged herself there and back. Then the next day Antie Liesbet told her to walk there again. So Susanna had started to walk every day. It had been three weeks now and she could feel herself getting stronger – much stronger than she had been for a long while. She had lost weight and her nails were growing back. Now since her trip to Colesberg, they had started having afternoon coffee together and Susanna had told her about Mom's gardens, about Dad who had grown up in Venda and about his sadness, like a poison, and how it makes her so angry. About Aunt Anna whom he loved so much. About all the letters and papers she found in the kist.

The old lady got up to fry the pumpkin in some fat and sugar. "You'll see. We're going to eat well."

She looked at Susanna. "Why don't you just phone him right now? Ask to speak to him directly. You'll feel much better."

Shooting monkeys

It's a beautiful day today, not like last week when it was Anna's birthday and we couldn't have a party with the other children because it rained the whole day. The sun is shining through the leaves and I'm sitting in the treehouse so I can read my new book, which Father brought with him from the camp library for me. It's all about the adventures of a German hunter in East Africa. The hunter's dog goes everywhere with him. It looks a lot like Asta, except, of course, it doesn't have three legs.

I can see Anna in the Holumbe's garden, but can't work out what she is doing. She's wearing her flower dress that Mutti made for her birthday and Mukegulu has tied Ella onto her back for her. There are so many butterflies around her. Earlier she asked me to help her move Djambo and all the things up to the Bester's graveyard, but I didn't feel like doing anything this morning other than read my book. Father announced at breakfast that he had asked Samuel to tidy up the front garden because he is expecting a visit from the Superintendent of the Mission Society in a few weeks time

Djambo is too heavy for Anna to move by herself and after a while I feel guilty and close the book. Then, just as I'm about to climb down the ladder to help her, a strange thing happens - the church bells start to ring. Nobody at the house seems to take much notice of them though. Mukegulu carries on sweeping the yard and Anna, who is now crouching next to a bush looking at something on the ground, only looks up briefly.

A swarm of bees flies by and I lie down flat on the platform so that I won't be stung, but the church bells ring again and I know this time it's to lure the monkeys out.

I want to laugh out loud, but then I see Father coming out of the house wearing one of Mutti's old dresses, the pale green one with the white flowers and the lace around the collar. He looks so funny. He has an old pair of slippers over his socks and a colourful scarf tied around his head. Just like the old witch in our book of fairy tales. I want to call out to Anna to look, but Father walks right under the tree with his rifle under his arm and I have to hold my mouth so that I don't make a noise. He heads for the orchard.

Then I remember the conversation between Mutti and him last night and I know he's going to shoot monkeys today.

He stands waiting for them behind a large guava tree.

Anna has found eggs under a bush, she picks them up and gathers them carefully in her skirt. I know she wants to take them to the chicken coop so that Asta doesn't eat them. She sees Mutti in the orchard and steps towards her. But it's Father and she doesn't know that. She's half hidden by the grass that is tall now from the rain. I see Father turn around and take aim. He thinks she is a monkey. He's is a good shot and she falls, still holding the eggs in her dress. She looks surprised.

I want to scream at him, but all I do is mumble, "She was just going to show you the eggs."

I lie down on my back. I never want to move from here again. Just stare at the sky forever.

Like Anna.

19.

When Susanna got back to her room, she sat down at the desk again and started to read through Grandfather's papers, but the autumn light kept coming in to disturb her. Maybe she should phone Dad. She got up and climbed up the little rocky outcrop, the only place on the farm you could get a decent cell phone signal. As long as she didn't start crying again. Grace had told her that Dad was crying a lot and imagine if she now also started - a duet.

She sat down on a stone to gather herself. From up here she could see the whitewashed house with smoke coming out of the chimney and her little cottage across the yard. She could look far across Oorlogspoort to the koppies from which sprung the fountain that brought them the water where the Fishwoman lived. There was a nip in the air and the evening light had turned everything into gold. The old windmill was clanking away next to her.

Grace always answered the phone immediately.

"How is he?" Susanna's heart beat unexpectedly fast.

"Wonderful." Grace sounded happy. "He's getting better every day. Just still a bit stubborn sometimes, but fine."

"Can I speak to him, you think?"

There was a pause and then she could hear his breathing on the phone.

"It's Susie, Pappie," Grace was coaxing him in the background.

"Hullo Dad," Susanna spoke loudly. "How are you?"

He was still breathing heavily.

"I've decided to come visit you for Easter, Dad. It'll be your birthday. You're turning 75."

He was trying to say something.

"Maybe we can hunt for Easter eggs," she laughed.

"Anna." It came out all strangled.

He was struggling to say her name.

"I know, Dad. I'm sorry about the fight we had."

"Anna," he tried again.

"I'm so sorry I just left you. I'm so confused about everything myself. But at least Grace is looking after you."

There was an awkward silence before he tried again.

"Anna."

"I'll see you soon, Dad," was all she could think to say.

Grace took the phone. "I think he wants to say something about someone called Anna," she explained.

Anna

Samuel and Father have carried Anna onto the back veranda. She is lying on a mattress covered with a blanket and Willie and I aren't allowed to go too near her. There isn't that much blood, just her hair is thicker and blacker than usual. Anna's eyes are wide open. She looks like Snow White. Mutti sits next to her, talking to her all the time, rubbing her hands to make her warm even though it's a hot day.

We wait for Doctor Talbot to come. I hear Father say we must put Anna in the slaughter room because it is cooler in there and I panic.

"You can't do that," I scream. "You're not allowed to!"

"Calm down, Hannes," Father says as he paces the veranda. "What's the matter with you?"

Finally Doctor Talbot arrives with the ambulance and Miss Talbot immediately takes Mutti into her arms.

Doctor Talbot examines Anna. He says he can't understand why she is still breathing and that it's a miracle that the bullet didn't kill her. They carry her to the ambulance. Mutti climbs into the back with her, but we aren't allowed to come with. Willie starts to cry, so VhoSarah takes us into the bedroom and closes the curtains and doors. We sit down on the bed and Mukegulu brings warm milk, honey and herbs.

"Vhafunzi says to tell you that everything will be all right," she says. "The hospital will make Anna better."

At last Willie calms down and I can hear voices coming from the kitchen veranda. When I ask her, Mukegulu tells me that it's the prayer women. They have come to sing and pray for Anna.

When Father and Mutti come back from Sibasa, I hear Father talking to the women and they leave soon afterwards. Mutti is upset with him.

"At least you should have let them pray for Anna," I hear her say.

"It's not as if she's dead," Father snaps.

Everything goes funny for a while and I can't remember much, just that we don't have school because Mutti isn't feeling well and that I don't have to have any more catechism classes.

One day VhoSarah comes into Anna and my's room with the linen bag. I'm lying on my bed reading, and she starts to pack Anna's things into the bag, shaking her head.

"These white people," she says crossly. "I told the Vhafunzi it's much too early to pack the child's things away. Her spirit won't want to come back to us. But he insists."

As she is about to take Anna's duvet off the bed, I leap across onto Anna's bed and hold onto the thick feather blanket, burying myself in it. "Don't take it away," I say.

"Sorry." VhoSarah sits down beside me.

"You shouldn't sleep in here alone, little Vhafunzi." She strokes my hair. "What do you say if I make Willie's bed here so he can sleep next to you?"

"I don't want Willie in here." I take Anna's duvet and pull it onto my bed. "He's just going to pee in Anna's bed and then the room will stink!"

Every night I wrap myself in Anna's blanket, breathing it in, looking for her smell. I hide Ella under my bed in case someone wants to take her away.

Doctor Talbot comes to visit. He goes straight into Mutti's room. When he comes out again, he looks very serious. Father takes Mutti to the clinic immediately.

"Is Mutti going to visit Anna?" asks Willie.

Mukegulu explains that the new baby in Mutti's stomach didn't want to grow anymore.

When Mutti comes back she is angry all the time and Father moves into the guest room for a while. Once or twice Mutti shouts at VhoSarah and Mukegulu for being lazy, but afterwards she always apologises to them. When I tell her that I don't want Willie to sleep in my bedroom, she slaps me and tells me to stop thinking only of myself. I remember how she hit Anna because Anna laughed at Father's story.

Mutti says that this year she can't face baking cakes for Christmas.

"We must all try to pull ourselves together," says Father. "Anna could get better."

But he is also sad, I can see that. He sits in his study a lot, doing nothing.

After New Year, Thambulo finally comes back from Nshelele. I'm very happy to see him because the next week I have to go to Pretoria to start proper school. I hang around Mukegulu's mudi and watch him carving things with his knife and he tells me about initiation school.

When we are tired we go to visit the Holumbe's garden. We decide to pick up Djambo and take him down to the graveyard at Old Wittenberg. No one is going to bother him there. The graveyard is overgrown; it must be a long time since anyone has come to clean the graves. Thambulo and I put down Djambo under the wild fig and sit next to him and relax for a while.

"Do you remember when we went into the old ruin and got such a fright because we thought we saw the Pythonman?" says Thambulo.

"But he was there, I saw him."

Thambulo keeps quiet.

"Do you think Anna is going to be alright?"

He looks at me.

"I should have warned her. I was sitting in the treehouse. I could see Father with his gun wearing Mutti's dress. He was going to shoot monkeys. I was laughing."

"Mukegulu says that some people say that Anna got shot because she's a monkey."

"Do you think that's true, Thambulo?"

Thambulo thinks for a while. "I don't really know," he says.

20.

That afternoon he must have slept very deeply because when he woke up everything was unusually quiet. All he could hear was the crackling of the house contracting as it cooled down. Not even the radio was playing in the kitchen. He wondered where Grace was. By this time she usually had washed him.

He heard muted voices in the kitchen. He strained to listen but he couldn't understand anything. Grace's voice was soothing and beseeching, the other more urgent and harsh. He had heard it somewhere before. Grace sounded upset. His heart sank. Maybe Pulane's mother had come to take her to Johannesburg with her, or maybe she wanted to send her to boarding school. He would not allow that. The child was happy here with her grandmother. He would provide for everything.

He heard footsteps in the passage making their way towards the front door. Grace was asking her guest to speak softly, but the woman stubbornly raised her voice. Johannes' heart beat faster. It was the rainmaker woman, the one who had been praying in front of his house. He had to see her, see whether she was okay. That her wounds were healing after the fire. Thank her for calling the rains. He had to check that Grace had shown her proper hospitality. Tell her about Thambulo who had come to visit him and how he had offered Thambulo his legs - she would understand these things. He reached for the bell next to the bed and shook it so hard that it fell to the ground.

Grace came running in.

"What is the matter, Pappie?" she said.

He pointed to the woman standing at the door now. She looked as strong and beautiful as ever, her skin unharmed by the fire, wearing the black mourning cape.

He tried to smile at her.

"This is my youngest sister, Pappie," said Grace. "Her name is Esther. I'm sorry if we woke you up. She's just had a lot of troubles."

He pointed at the water next to the bed, tried to lift his hands to show rain, but she didn't understand.

"Do you need water?"

Johannes patted the bed.

"He wants you to sit down next to him."

The woman looked at him suspiciously.

"My sister just lost her son," Grace said. "He was shot."

"I'm so sorry," he tried to mouth. "So sorry." He looked at Grace, hoping she would understand and interpret for him.

The phone rang in the kitchen. "It's probably Susanna calling again." Grace looked at her watch.

The woman sat down reluctantly on the visitor's chair next to the window and looked at him blankly. After a while she turned her head and stared outside into the dusk.

Then she said, "He was shot by the police. I didn't even know he was making bad things. Stealing cars."

So her name was Esther.

"Did Grace tell you that my husband was an MK soldier? That was the problem. The boy never knew his father."

He wished she would sit closer so he could look at her properly. It was a miracle that the fire hadn't harmed her.

"Grace probably didn't tell you either that when we were children our mother used to work in this house." She looked at him again.

He shook his head.

"They had big black dogs, the Ferreiras. We used to sit under those blue gums over there and wait for Mama to go on break so she could come and sit with us. Sometimes Mrs Ferreira would try to chase us away or she would stand on the veranda and scold Mama."

She got up and stood looking out of the window. "Did you know that that's old Mr Ferreira's car out there? The old Cortina. He crashed it right in front of his own house.' Her laugh was dry and bitter. "He worked for the municipality and he used to drink a lot. He crashed into those trees and died on the spot. It's funny that no one ever removed the wreck."

Grace must have forgotten to come back. She had stopped speaking on the phone for a while already.

"When Mrs Ferreira sold the place, Mama couldn't find work. So Grace left school to go and find work in Johannesburg to support us." He could see a slight resemblance to Grace now. She was younger though and had sad eyes.

"When we lived in Botswana I used to dream about this place all the time, dreaming that I was waiting under the trees for Mama." The dusk was turning the room red. Esther's sadness was making him thirsty.

"Even when I came back, I still dreamt of waiting for Mama there." Her voice softened. "And while I was dreaming, my son was running with those dogs."

There was a long silence. Johannes closed his eyes. The sadness was darkening the room, pressing onto his chest, burning. He wondered when Grace would come back.

Her voice was tired now. "You must sleep, Pappie,' she said.

She sat down next to him on the bed. He opened his eyes. She was beautiful, like VhoSarah. He wanted to tell her how sorry he was - about her mother and her son. He wanted to tell her that she must come and live here with them. When he was gone, they could all stay on if they wanted to. He would ask Jooste to put in the borehole so that they could make a garden and plant fruit trees and vegetables. They could sell them to the people walking along the path. They could chop down those old blue gums, like Susanna had always wanted him to do, and plant shade trees in the yard. For the people to sit under.

Boarding school

And then it was time to pack my things for school. Mutti helped me and she said that I was lucky because I was going to be living close to Anna. At some time they had moved her to a big hospital in Pretoria where they were going to see if they could take the bullet out of her spine. Mutti didn't say anything when I gave her Anna's duvet and Ella to pack for me.

Father drove me to Evening Star so that I could get a lift with Uncle Els to Pretoria. The trip took all day and Missionary Els dropped me off at the hostel when it was already dark. He introduced me to the hostel mother, Mrs Botha, and wished me well.

There were fifteen beds in the dormitory, but most of the other boys were only going to arrive the next day. The room smelled of margarine and urine and the windows were very high. One other boy had already moved into the dormitory but I ignored him. The first thing I did was take the stiff grey blankets and green bedspread off my bed, and replace them with Anna's duvet. The boy started saying something but I didn't understand him. His hair was short and spiky. He pointed at the duvet and shook his head. I ignored him and quickly unpacked all my things into the small cupboard. VhoSarah had given me ginger cookies in a tin and I hid Ella behind them.

When I was done, I walked down the long passage to look for Mrs Botha. I found her sitting in an office like Father's, drinking a cup of tea.

"When can I visit my sister?" I asked her. Then I realised that she didn't understand English so well.

"I want to visit my sister, Anna," I tried again. "She is in a special hospital here in Pretoria and I have something I have to bring her."

Mrs Botha said something that sounded a bit like German but I couldn't understand it. Then she put down her teacup and rang a bell and took me to the dining room. I didn't feel much like eating the grey soup and strange white bread, but I tried.

After supper I walked across the grass to the big building where Missionary Els had dropped off Wilfried and Conrad. I was a bit scared of going inside but finally I walked through the door. The place was full of big boys who were shouting and scrapping and it was all very noisy. Some said funny things to me, but then I found Wilfried.

"I want to visit Anna," I told him. "You have to come with me and explain to Mrs Botha because she can't understand English or Tshivenda."

The boys around him laughed and started to imitate my voice, making up singsong German. Wilfried quickly took me outside, away from them. He was thinking very hard.

"Maybe you must write a letter to your father so that he can write to the school so that they can organise for you to go and visit Anna."

I looked at him blankly. "I just want to bring her Ella, I think she will like that."

"You know, Hannes," Wilfried said as he started walking me back to my hostel. "Here at school you can't just walk around at night whenever you want to. Just now Mrs Botha is going to lock up the hostel for the night and then you'll be in big trouble."

He left me at the entrance of my hostel and the next day I wrote a letter to Father. I don't know if he ever got it because he never sent a reply.

21.

The house was getting very busy. There seemed to be people coming and going all day long. The big gate opened and closed often and there was a constant crunch of footsteps on the gravel path. Maybe he should speak to Susanna about it when she came to visit him. And the incessant talking - all the way up the stairs, right outside his room on the veranda and then more talking over tea in the kitchen.

He didn't mind so much that Grace's youngest son had moved in recently, he would have preferred to have her sister here but Grace said that she needed someone to help her lift and carry him. He could understand that. Mpho was apparently sleeping on the sofa in the lounge, and somehow the thought of Mutti and Father watching the young man cheered Johannes up a bit. But then he remembered that Susanna had taken the picture down.

Grace said that Mpho would be useful if she needed to go out sometimes. He really didn't like that idea at all. He could see that the young man wasn't too happy with washing and lifting him onto the bedpan, but there was nothing either of them could do about it. They were stuck with each other for a while.

Mpho was a quiet and sullen young man and Grace was always saying that she wished he would go and re-do his matric so that he could learn something and find a proper job.

Today there seemed to be more goings on than usual in the kitchen. Judging by the hymns on the radio, it was Sunday and Grace was cooking meat and pap. He wished she would make him a nice sharp peanut sauce with spinach, like Mukegulu used to.

He could hear Pulane playing outside on the veranda. She was a solitary child, talking to herself all the time. Pulane's mother still wanted to send the little girl to an expensive boarding school so that she could learn English, but her grandmother had fought against it.

"A child needs love more than a fancy education. The white school in Stillefontein will be good enough for her," Grace had said.

A car hooted at the gate. The little girl jumped out of the rocking chair: "Gogo! Gogo!" she called to her grandmother.

Maybe Susanna was coming to see him. It was high time. He needed to talk to her. Or maybe it was Esther again.

But then he heard the familiar voice of the physiotherapist and his body went limp with disappointment. He wanted to protest that he didn't need her today, especially on a Sunday, but of course she soon was all over him with her ridiculous energy and the smell of disinfectant.

"I brought you a surprise, Mr Weber," Miss du Plooy beamed. "A wheelchair!"

He didn't see why he needed a wheelchair but Grace seemed happy as well.

"Batho, Mr Weber, now we can take you out onto the veranda every day."

All this fussing.

"Susanna," he protested.

"Yes," Grace said. "She organised it for you."

When they lifted him out of the bed, he tried to make his body rigid. But it didn't help. Before long they had him in the chair and Miss du Plooy, efficient as ever, had put a blanket over his knees and pushed him towards the door. Couldn't they just leave him alone?

When he got outside, the daylight was so bright that he had to close his eyes.

After a while he opened them again. And then he saw the veld. It had turned bright green, and there were flowers. How did this happen? The koppies were luminous with freshness. How could it have rained and he hadn't even noticed? Esther must have brought the rain.

The birds - he had completely forgotten about them. They were waiting for him on the fence and on the peach trees whose leaves had already turned yellow and orange. Easter - it would be Easter soon. His birthday sometime. Susanna had said so. The cosmos was tall and pink and white along the road, hiding the old car wreck.

Johannes turned towards Grace. They were all standing around him, looking at him.

"Don't worry, Pappie," Grace reassured him. "We'll leave you out here for a while. We're going to have lunch in the kitchen. I've cooked Miss du Plooy a proper African meal."

They went inside and Johannes closed his eyes again. He wanted to feel the cool breeze against his skin.

Father used to say: "God does not live in the forest and in the rivers, God lives in heaven." How could he have said such a thing? How did he never see how beautiful everything really was - people walking past, and the clouds moving across the clear blue sky? And the green. He had to find Esther and thank her.

He must have drifted off because when he opened his eyes again, Pulane was standing next to him, holding her plate of food. He wondered how long she had been there looking at him. She offered him a small ball of pap, dipped in sauce. He opened his mouth and accepted it. Delicious. Then she sat down on the rocking chair next to him and quietly ate her food. She gazed out across the green veld and up to where the koppies held the horizon. Now and again she fed him morsels from her plate. He longed to tell her about the rheebuck that Susanna had seen up there. Go up into the koppies with her and wait for them in the grove of sweet thorns.

He had fallen asleep again and when he woke up he was glad that no one had taken him back inside. The swallows were gathering on the razor wire, striped swallows. He counted at least twenty-six. Must be getting ready to migrate already, maybe they would fly over Tanzania. Maybe to Germany, to Berlin.

Pulane was standing near the fence making silver patterns with the hosepipe, shrieking when one of the big drops fell onto her. The birds didn't seem to mind her. They sat on the fence and in the trees, waiting. He saw one or two swoop through the stream of water, drinking. The child had a habit of offering water to everybody who passed by. Some accepted, others ignored her or just chatted for a bit. Mostly they eyed Johannes suspiciously, but Pulane would gesture towards the veranda as if to say, "Don't worry about him, he can't do anything to you."

When Susanna came to visit at Easter, he would ask her to make a bed of roses. She would know which ones Kate liked. That would be nice. He would be able to look at them from up here.

Later he saw a group of children peeping into the old car wreck. Pulane tried her best to spray them through the fence but they were too far away. She waited patiently with her hosepipe and then, as soon as they came closer, she sprayed them. It wasn't long before they slipped through the open gate and started to join in the fun.

Johannes was about to call Grace to come and chase away the children - they were getting noisy and wasting water - but then he saw it. At first he thought it was a swallow coming to join the others. Then he thought it was a see-through plastic bag blowing over the razor wire. It came closer and he recognised the effervescent colours and the clumsy flight. It swooped by close and winked at him.

"Look," he tried to shout to the children. "Look, there's the Holumbe!"

It flew right in amongst them as they were stripping off their clothes and jumping through the water. But the children didn't notice. They were too busy chasing the stream of water and screaming with pleasure as the heavy drops fell onto their hot skins. Grace had brought out the old tin bath and Pulane was filling it with water so that they could all swim in it.

The Holumbe perched itself on a branch of the peach tree right above them. Pulane pulled her tongue out at it and it turned its bum to her and made a big soap bubble. Johannes wanted to clap his hands with joy. The Holumbe saw this and immediately came flying up to him, beckoning him to follow it.

"I can't," he tried to explain. "I've had a stroke."

The Holumbe just laughed and continued to beckon him. He wanted so badly to follow it. It flew to the razor fence and blew itself into all kinds of shapes to entice him. He could feel his body strain with longing. He wanted to follow it into the veld and look at the flowers that had come up after the rain and wait for the mountain rheebuck.

"Batho, Mr Weber!" It was Grace. She was standing next to him with the cell phone in her hands. "You'll fall if you do that."

Johannes sat back and watched the Holumbe vanish into the

veld.

"Susanna wants to talk to you again."

22

Everything looked so different from the last time she was here. The drought had just broken then and the veld was still brown and strained - and now all this lushness and the tall pink and white cosmos and the grasses swaying with ripeness. She had had to fight so hard to get Dad out of hospital and organise everything – regular home visits by the physio and the GP, medical aid payments for home care, throwing things away, making space for Grace – the angel of grace, offering to move in with Pulane to look after him. She had even put the Berlin furniture onto the train to Pretoria to Uncle Willie, who had muttered gentle protestations over the phone at her but she just couldn't think what else to do - she had been so tired, so insufferably tired and unfit and miserable.

She could already see from the outside that the house and garden were spotless. The little girl opened the gate and led her up the steep veranda stairs where Grace was waiting for her.

"How is he?" She could feel the tears rising.

Grace hugged her. "He is tired and he doesn't open his eyes much."

Someone had picked cosmos and put it in vases in all the rooms.

"It's Ntate Johannes' birthday today," said the child.

"I know. That's why I came. And on Sunday it's Easter and I brought you and Dad lots of Easter Eggs and cookies and condensed milk."

Pulane clapped her hands and then became serious again. "Do you know that Ntate Johannes can speak Tshivenda and German and English and Afrikaans?"

The sun was shining through the pink curtains of the front room. He looked so small lying there amongst the white pillows. His hair, still dark, had grown long and wispy around his face. He looked almost like a woman, like Auntie Anna just before she died. She must ask Grace to cut it.

"Hullo Dad," she said and bent down to kiss him on the forehead.

He smiled softly, his eyes remaining closed.

"You can sit down next to him," Grace said.

"What about all these pipes and things?"

"It's fine. He likes it when you sit next to him. Hold his hand."

His hand was under the duvet and a drip was hanging off his arm. Painful sobs pushed up through her. "He's bad isn't he?"

"He's a bit better today. I think it's because he knew you were coming."

"Do we need to take him back to the hospital?"

"He's much better here. We take him outside onto the veranda sometimes in the wheelchair."

She found his hand. He pressed hers. There were tears running down his cheeks.

"He's happy to see you."

His olive skin had become so thin and translucent. She had always envied his skin. Why did she have to inherit so much from Grandfather – all that sensitivity and the freckles? It wasn't fair.

Dad once told her that when Grandfather came back from the camp he had been concerned that his and Anna's skin had gone too dark. "You must keep them out of the sun, Elisabeth, this way people won't know who their father is," he had said. Dad had giggled when he told her the story, such a sweet childish giggle. Like Auntie Anna in the nursing home playing with her fingers, making shapes, and giggling and making odd sounds.

"Happy birthday, Dad." He did not respond.

"I stopped in Bloemfontein to get us some Jerepigo and lots of Easter eggs – marshmallow ones and the hollow ones you like. Maybe we can sit in the garden and hide them for Grace's granddaughter." He squeezed her hand again. Such a lovely smile he had. Why had he used it so seldom?

"Anna." His voice was strange and muffled.

"Pulane and I are going to make you tea and when you are ready you can join us in the kitchen," said Grace.

"Can I have coffee? With condensed milk?"

"Anna," he said again.

"Who is Anna?" Grace asked.

"It's his sister. She was a paraplegic. She was shot by their dad. It was a mistake. She lived in a nursing home in Pretoria for thirty years."

"Batho, I first thought it was you. He says her name all the time." Grace hugged Pulane against her. "Poor man!"

Susanna pushed a long strand of hair out of his face. "Mom and I used to visit her often, but Dad never wanted to come with us."

Despite the urine bag, the room smelled fresh and clean. "Why was that, Dad?"

Grace left the room.

"I found your letters to Auntie Anna in the kist."

He opened his eyes and looked at her.

"When I was at university Mom and I used to wonder where you were going all the time. Why didn't you tell us you were visiting her?"

He shrugged his shoulders and closed his eyes again.

"I said to Mom that you were having an affair, but she said that was nonsense."

He smiled. She didn't want to start crying again, not in front of him. It would only upset him. She got up.

"Tonight we'll celebrate your birthday. I'm going to feed you Jerepigo with a spoon and we can play Gospel music."

Grace had already carried the tray outside onto the veranda. The little girl was sitting on the rocking chair. She held out a plate with thick slices of bread with jam and cheese and sausages. Susanna declined.

"Didn't they feed you in Karoo? You've lost so much weight."

Susanna told Grace about Antie Liesbet who made her walk far every day, and eat healthy food, and about the beautiful farm with its bushes and medicinal plants and the kist full of letters and documents.

"Are you going to move there?"

"I don't know, Antie Liesbet's daughter Althea is coming to visit me here. I'll see what happens."

They were quiet for a while, looking out onto the veld together. Pulane started rocking on Dad's chair.

"Have you seen any snakes around?"

Grace shook her head.

"How long does he still have?"

"You can never tell. People come on such long roads, you can never tell."

23

For days the Holumbe hovered about, calling him into the veld. Finally he managed to follow it. Anna joined them.

They struggled to keep up with it as it zigzagged wildly from rock to grass to rock to bush to grass to rock to bush. When they finally reached the clump of sweet-thorns, they all sat down to catch their breaths.

"Susanna has seen a pair of mountain rheebuck somewhere here,' he told Anna.

"I wish we could see them too," she said.

Johannes was so happy that she was back. He wanted to ask her many questions. He wanted to know where she had been, what she had seen.

He noticed that the Holumbe was playing with a Silversnake, so he bent down to pick up a stone.

"What are you doing?" asked Anna.

"That's a snake."

"Don't throw it with a stone, you'll kill it."

"But it will bite the Holumbe," he protested.

"It won't! It won't!" She sounded panicked.

"But it's a snake."

"Don't. Please don't." She was close to tears now. "Just leave it, Hannes."

"Okay," he said and put down the stone again.

She smiled, relieved and before he could say anything else, Anna jumped up and took his hand and pulled at him.

"I know what we'll do," she said. "Let's lie down here and let the snake crawl over us."

"You're mad, Anna. What if it bites us?"

"It won't. You'll see." She pulled him down onto the ground next to her. The sweet-thorns were in full bloom after the rain and the bees and other insects feasted on the sweet yellow balls. The ground was cool and moist and Johannes shut his eyes tightly, waiting for the creature to slide over him.

Anna squeezed his hand. "Are your eyes open?"

"No," he whispered, breathing in her familiar smell.

"Mine neither," she giggled.

"Maybe we should open them."

Acknowledgements

Thank you to the Johannsmeier family for taking me around Venda, sharing letters and photographs, and opening up the stories of your childhood on the beautiful mission station, Georgenholz, at Makonde. The hours of conversations with your mother, Thea Johannsmeier, Annegret's tale of the garden and her experience of her father's return from the internment camp, inspired this story. *Shooting Snakes* is a figment of my imagination and in no way depicts your hardworking and loving parents.

Then, of course, there was my mother with her vivid sense of the 'story' in history. A few years ago she handed over her valuable collection of mission reports and history to me and I wish I could put a copy of this book into her hands.

In 2004 and 2005 I was fortunate to be part of the British Council Crossing Borders programme which mentored writers from Southern Africa. Catherine Johnson and Kath McKay acted as skilful and patient midwives to this book and helped sharpen the tools of the craft. The programme provided such a vital dose of confidence for this long journey and I wish it could be reinstated.

Dr Godfrey Dederen from the University of Venda gave me copies of precious documents on the world of the Vhavenda and accompanied me to Georgenholz for a second visit. He brought alive the spirit world and roped in his wife, Onika, to check the spelling and usage of Tshivenda words. Any mistakes that slipped through are not her fault.

Thank you so much to Teacher Ratshilumela from Georgenholz Primary for taking me to meet some of the elders of Makonde so that I could ask them about the missionaries who had lived in their midst. And to the girls who showed me the beautiful tshigombela dance.

Dr Lize Kriel, thank you for taking me with you to Germany to meet church historians and for introducing me to the work of Alan Kirkaldy, *Capturing the Soul, The Vhavenda and the missionaries, 1870 – 1900*.

Ina le Roux in her kitchen in Parkhurst shared the story of the rabbit Sankampe who, one by one, ate all the lion cubs.

A very special thank you to David Medalie for his unstinting generosity and discernment - what a luck to be in your writing group and to have your friendship! To all the other members of the group, thank you for listening and being such a brilliant sounding board.

Thank you also to Gisela Winkler and Angifi Dladla for reading through the raw manuscript.

Nella Freund, you are a dream editor and we need lots more like you in this country.

Colleen Higgs, power to your press!

Beverley Naidoo, my writing friend, thank you for your deep wisdom, skill and support.

Elza Miles, you are the medicine woman to my creative endeavours.

Alex Hassett and that terrible Missing-Each-Other are co-creators of the Holumbe.

Thank you to my dear friend with the sharp eye, Frances Williams, for giving everything a good proofing at the end - and for your generous support throughout.

Graeme Williams, thank you for taking pictures. I hereby absolve you from any accusations that I look old.

And Mervyn, thank you for marrying me in all of this.

Other fiction titles by Modjaji Books

Love Interrupted
by **Reneilwe Malatji**

Bom Boy
by **Yewande Omotos**

Snake
by **Tracey Farren**

Whiplash
by **Tracey Farren**

Go Tell the Sun
by **Wame Molefhe**

The Bed Book of Short Stories
edited by **Joanne Hichens**

The Thin Line
by **Arja Salafranca**

This Place I Call Home
by **Meg Vandermerwe**

www.modjajibooks.co.za

"In Shooting Snakes the past is a powerful and insistent presence. In the beguiling rhythms of the narrative, its carefully plotted to-and-fro chronology, lies a profound understanding of the vexed relationship between past and present. In this skilfully wrought novel, Maren Bodenstein brings to light a little-known aspect of South African history."

- David Medalie